DEFINITIONS
OF A HORSE

DEFINITIONS
OF A HORSE

Jaci Stephen

To George and Gill,
Best wishes,
Jaci Stephen

13.10.90

Hutchinson

LONDON   SYDNEY   AUCKLAND   JOHANNESBURG

This edition first published in 1990 by
Hutchinson

Random Century Ltd,
20 Vauxhall Bridge Road, London SW1V 2SA

Random Century Australia (Pty) Ltd
20 Alfred Street, Milsons Point, NSW 2061, Australia

Random Century New Zealand Limited
PO Box 40–086, Glenfield, Auckland 10, New Zealand

Random Century South Africa (Pty) Ltd
PO Box 337, Bergvlei, 2012 South Africa

British Library Cataloguing in Publication Data
Stephen, Jaci
  Definitions of a horse.
  I. Title
  823'.914

  ISBN 0–09–174425–3

Photoset by Speedset Ltd, Ellesmere Port
Printed and bound in Great Britain by
Butler & Tanner Ltd, Frome, Somerset

For Bevis Hillier
and
In Memory of My Father

The author wishes to acknowledge the financial assistance of the Welsh Arts Council and the overdraft facilities of Lloyds Bank, Queen Street, Cardiff.

'Girl number twenty unable to define a horse!' said Mr Gradgrind, for the general behoof of all the little pitchers. 'Girl number twenty possessed of no facts, in reference to one of the commonest of animals.'

Hard Times
Charles Dickens

CONTENTS

CHAPTER ONE

BREEDS AND TYPES: BREAKING IN

HEAVY DRAUGHT: Physically very strong.
SHIRE: Descendant of the Old English War Horse.
CLYDESDALE: Strong, though less weighty than the Shire.
Hard wearing feet and legs, good elasticated movement.
SUFFOLK: Enormous neck and square body.
PERCHERON: Tall, strong, with wide, docile eyes and an
intelligent expression.

The Deputy Head had enjoyed his summer vacation. He had
read *Anna Karenina* again and put together a collection of his
own poems based upon his experience of tunnels. Life is one
long series of tunnels, he said in the preface: mine shafts, the
Underground, British Rail; and each was a symbol of the Great
Tunnel of Love and Life. It was essential to enter the darkest of
tunnels if mankind were to be saved. Only in the blackness of
despair can Man fully come to realize his inner potential and
thus re-enter the light. Harold Graystone explained his theory
to friends in the Lake District where he had spent the greater
part of his holiday. Now he was returning in a state of
intoxicated pleasure, anticipating a productive term. He had
memorised up to (and including) line 376 of *The Prelude*; after
all, 'A man's real possession is his memory', as he told his
pupils. He forgot to tell them the quotation was not his own.
Testing a passionate delivery of the lines against the autumn
wind as he cycled to school, he managed to reach 'I might
endue some airy phantasies' as his front wheel passed the
freshly painted yellow school gates.

1

He wheeled his bicycle to the dark wooden sheds (remembering, for the twenty-fifth year, that cycling was forbidden on school premises) and chained his new machine (he would keep in better shape this year) in the corner designated for him alone. He cast a warning stare at some small newcomers, doubtless eyeing up the possibilities of the traditional hideout.

'Remember this area is strictly out of bounds, except to those who bring bicycles to school,' he warned. Better to start off strictly and ease up later on. 'And don't chew gum, lad.' The boys wandered away and giggled as a large, damp leaf floated down and anointed the shining bald head of Graystone. He put his hand to his head, removed the sign and thought again of Wordsworth.

Dressed in a blue cycling suit, he slid out from behind the large oak tree that guarded the bike sheds, and surveyed the grounds. Enormous trees, a shrivelled green, showed evidence of a long, hot summer. Stumps of others that had been cut down revealed the decay of Dutch Elm disease. Chestnut trees lined the playing fields, heavy with conkers in the first stages of growth. Doubtless there would be the usual period of conker bashing, or whatever the young hooligans called it these days. Graystone remembered his own boyhood and the joys of hunting for the hard green cases among the leaves; coming upon one unexpectedly, splitting the skin to discover the perfect shine of a conker; the excitement in extracting it from its white cushion, discovering the brown pearl to be bigger than all the others in his collection; a large creamy eye staring boldly and ready for attack. The caretaker would already be rehearsing his annual ritual of complaints, assuring Graystone that this time he would definitely not believe where he had discovered conker chippings. Desks, showers, toilets, keyholes, nostrils; no orifice was sacred. Graystone sighed. 'Ah, season of myths and meadow fruitfulness,' he recited, on an exaggerated inbreath of air.

Graystone loved the waxy smell of corridors and polish that greeted his arrival on the first day of each new term. He stumbled into school through the main door, burdened with charts, posters and magazines. In the absence of mental agility, he was a great believer in visual aids. He had built up quite a supply over the years, particularly during the period when he had been made Acting Head of English. He liked to make it clear that he still maintained an active interest in the welfare of the department.

The staff room had not changed. Graystone rarely visited the one at the 'old' side of the school, the Junior Common Room. That one was for the more frivolous teachers who were under the illusion that nothing carried credence unless it was conveyed by many thousands of decibels. They were drawn to it by instinct within their first hour of entering the school. Graystone's preference was for the company of the less raucous Senior Common Room members. Here, too, was where notices and timetables were pinned up, the argument being that it was strategically more convenient for the secretaries to keep staff up to date on the latest developments in the outside world.

Graystone deposited his case and drew on the pile of information that had accumulated in his absence. 'Now let me see,' he said, addressing a yellow sheet of paper. 'Oh, yes . . .' hm . . . well, I don't know about that.' He disposed of a green sheet, an invitation to join a Contemporary Dance class. Each sheet was more colourful than the last. Some he delivered into other pigeon holes. New members of staff were always pleased to receive an overflow of diaries, booklets and preparation material, and if Graystone could add a little something to make them feel more at home, he would. He posted a form into 'Postlethwaite', a course on *Anglo-Saxon for Teenagers*, the latest County contribution to their *Make English Interesting* campaign.

Timothy Leach stretched up on tip-toe in front of the bathroom mirror and tugged at the green and white tie knotted around his throat. As he wrenched it apart for the fourth time, his face turned red with frustration as the material, growing in abundance with each attempt, twisted his small fingers. Finally, he made a loose heart around one fist and passed the loop with painstaking care over his head, bowing like an Olympic medallist receiving an award on the rostrum. He edged the knot once more towards his shirt collar and with a little pulling and stretching was able to cover a good seventy degrees of the grey angle, held geometrically in place by a small white button. For a brief moment, pride overcame fear, and Timothy went cheerfully downstairs to breakfast.

3

'You're up early,' said his father, entering the kitchen.

Timothy was halfway through a bowl of corn flakes. He managed a milky 'mmm' in response.

'What on earth's that?' asked Derek Leach, indicating his son's tie. 'Come here.' He leaned over to unravel the knot. 'There. That's better.'

'Dad . . .' said Timothy, gazing thoughtfully into his milk. '. . . What if . . . What if I don't like it?'

His father laughed. 'Don't be silly. Everyone likes school.'

'Sheila didn't.'

'Sheila didn't what?' asked Timothy's elder sister, joining the family at the table.

'Like school,' repeated Timothy.

'Yes, she did, didn't you?' emphasized the father, giving his daughter a conspiratorial wink.

'Well . . .'

'There you are. Nothing to worry about. Everybody likes school.'

'I hated it,' said Sheila. 'For weeks. Months.' She avoided the thwarted look she knew would, by now, have appeared on her father's face. 'But it's like a lot of things. When we start them, they seem awful. But then we get used to them. In a few weeks, you'll wonder why ever you were worried – when you've made new friends and started subjects you've never done before.'

Timothy brightened. 'I'll get my things.'

He went upstairs to his bedroom to check again the inside of his stiff and shiny leather satchel. It smelt of newness and he fingered each of its contents in turn: the unscratched, transparent geometry equipment; the long, cleanly shaven pencils; the rainbow keyboard of crayons.

'Have you got your dinner-money?' asked his father, when Timothy re-entered the kitchen.

'Mmm,' he answered.

Rebecca, Timothy's younger sister, was sitting at the table. She looked up briefly before bombing her sugar puffs with a spoon. Timothy stood, awaiting recognition.

'Quite a little man,' said Mr Leach, subjecting his son's tie to further maltreatment. 'Turn around.'

Timothy made an awkward circular movement, struggling

4

with a satchel largely out of proportion to his undeveloped frame. 'I'll get my coat,' he said, and returned, wearing a black duffle coat four sizes too big for him. His father said he would grow into it.

'What's your name?'
'Melissa.'
'Melissa what?'
'Melissa Scotts.'
The two girls stood in the middle of the yard, each staring at the other as if she were an unknown species.
'What's yours?
'Charmaine Doberman.'
Melissa was uncertain as to whether she really wanted a friend with such a name. The girl had very large ears, too. She herself might come to be known as 'the friend of the girl with big ears'. Charmaine had even bigger doubts. Why did her potential playmate have the misfortune to possess a name like Melissa Scotts, when her enormous brace meant that every 's' was accompanied by a shower of spittle.
'What school do you come from?'
'Crabtree,' said Melissa.
'I don't.'
'Oh.'
'Don't you want to know where I went?'
Melissa did not. She had most definitely decided against the Doberman girl. Wasn't there a Smith or a Jones somewhere? But then – 'All right.' She had better play for time.
'I went to boarding school.'
'What's your name?' Melissa pounced on a new possibility.
'Janet Evans.'
Melissa smiled. 'Will you go around with me?'
Janet beamed gratefully. Charmaine Doberman growled and padded quietly away.

'You can tell they're only first years,' said Julia Summers, Form Two.
'We were never like that,' said her friend.

5

'You can't be in our gang unless you say the password,' said Ruth Gribble.

'Don't want to, anyway.'

'Bet you don't even know what the password is.'

'Don't want to.'

'It's . . .' Ruth Gribble whispered into Charmaine Doberman's ear. 'If you say it out loud, you can join.'

'I'm not allowed to say words like that.'

'Cissy! Cissy!'

'I'll spell it, though.'

Ruth frowned. She was not sure whether spelling counted. After all, swearing showed that you were really grown up. Neither was she certain how to spell the word; so even if she did allow a breach of the rules, Charmaine might be gaining admittance under false pretences.

'No,' she decided.

'Barstand,' said Charmaine, quickly.

'You didn't say it properly.'

'Yes I did.'

'Oh, all right. Cross your heart in hope to die, you'll serve our gang and never spy.'

Charmaine crossed.

'Why are you so short?' Leon Grimes, Form Four, approached Timothy Leach.

Timothy blinked and felt himself shrinking in the taller boy's presence.

'You new here?'

Timothy nodded.

'Well I'd be careful if I was you . . . because . . .' The boy leaned over, as if to impart a secret. '. . . Because at break, you'll be ducked in the toilet and what will your pretty hair look like then, eh?' Grimes ruffled the smaller boy's hair. 'And Mummy'll be vewy vewy angwy, won't she?' he laughed.

'My mother's . . . I haven't got a mother,' said Timothy.

'Left you all on uz own-ums, has she? Ah, diddums.'

'She's . . . She's dead,' said Timothy. But the boy had run off. 'She's dead,' he whispered again. It was the first time he had said the word aloud. 'Dead dead dead dead dead.' He repeated it until it became numb on the air and lost its meaning. Then

6

each monosyllable rose, joined, and finally fell, heavy with the single weight of their individual sounds. Dead.

'Blazer! . . . Jewellery! . . . Uniform!' shouted Grace Calne, marching stiffly across the yard. Her orders were aimed at groups rather than individuals, and were based upon the premise that just as every group contained a leader, each also possessed one pupil without a blazer, one wearing jewellery and one with the wrongly coloured socks. Her thirty-year teaching career had been spent in cultivating the art of speaking little in the hope of meaning much; hence the effectiveness, in her opinion, of single word demands. She prided herself upon the Biblical approach to language that, under temporal circumstances, was hers alone. The readings she chose for morning assembly always demonstrated such economy and she felt a great affinity with those characters who used words in the same manner as herself; statements of enormous philosophical significance, delivered with the utmost simplicity: 'Let there be light.' 'Be still and know that I am God.'

Grace Calne had been Senior Mistress at Riverside for five years. Her ascension to the role had been a slow one. It was only when she discovered the meaning of masturbation that she was able to prove her skills as an investigator of children's crime: reporting every instance in which she heard the activity mentioned in its glorious four-syllabled entirety, or else referred to by some less ambitious slang word. Her coup d'état came when, during a Christmas Carol Service, she sabotaged a plan by first year boys who had been planning a rather too literal enactment of 'O Come All Ye Faithful'. She was not called the Wanking Queen for nothing.

'I dare you to ask her if she's a virgin,' said a second year to his friend.

'Get lost.'

'Her husband died from a fish bone stuck in his throat . . . *honest*.'

'She had an evil stepmother.'

'She's got V.D.'

Andrew Young, Head of History, stood at the window of the

7

main staff room. 'The trouble with that woman,' he said, nodding towards Grace, 'is that she needs a damn good screw.'

At the age of fifty, Kenneth Salmon regarded his penis as an extra-terrestrial. He had hoped that they might have grown old together, gracefully, each anticipating the other's needs by instinct, like two old friends no longer having to rely upon the normal modes of communication. The penis had different ideas and was both looking and feeling its two score years and ten. There had to be more to life than this.

Salmon rested his legs against the toilet bowl as he tried to inspire his flaccid organ to what it damn well knew he was after. It gave him no encouragement, rejecting his advances like a close pal who, upon promotion to form captain, spurns his old circle of friends.

It was strange, really, having to try at all these days. For decades he had taken his early morning erections for granted: looked forward to them like he did the picture-cards in the packets of P.G. Tips at breakfast. With equal enthusiasm, he had dragged both from their hiding places, each still bearing the smell of stale captivity; examined them with the same microscopic attention to detail, looking for distinguishing marks and unusual features: a pimple here, the mast of a ship there; wrinkles and waves; grey hairs and gathering clouds. As long as the pictures continued to emerge, safe and clean from behind the foil, so his penis managed to greet the morning with a smile.

The stiffness would always be there when he woke – regular as cockwork. 'Miracle' was the only word that came to mind. Every morning, it was as if he were experiencing a revelation, being Born Again; feeling, at last, as if he had come to understand God's motive. The Bible stories were based upon the Erection Principle: the joy of watching the little become much. Water into wine at the marriage of Cana; Noah's capacity for animal magic; bread and fish at the feeding of the five thousand. And, until recently, he had never experienced the post-coital drain that men were supposed to feel. Twelve baskets of leftovers? He could have filled twelve dozen.

Ha! Those were the days. Now, he set a time limit on it: if it

8

wasn't there by the time he got around to cleaning his teeth, he gave up.

This morning was one of those days. He let go of his penis as if it were a glove puppet for which the operator has lost enthusiasm. He thought he heard it sigh as it flopped; relieved, at last, to be laid to rest. Choosing a clean pair of underpants from a drawer – always black on days of mourning – Salmon pulled them up carefully over his genitals, concealing his treasure with the delicacy and affection with which he imagined Harry Corbett once packed Sooty into his holiday suitcase.

It was at times like this that he thought of the bizarre nature of Doing It. How strange that people were Doing It all the time. Right this minute in fact, there were hundreds, thousands, millions of people with their legs spread wide: doing unto others, being done by. It wasn't fair. Millions of arms and legs contorted backwards, upside down, side to side in an attempt to salvage what might otherwise have been just another one of those days. He could smell the sweat and sperm of their bodies as this world choir of orgasmic yells echoed in his head; a room of human clocks, set to chime the hour at two second intervals apart. Each new image produced another like the inescapable picture of eternity he used to imagine as a child: the nightmare of watching, listening, feeling for evermore, a *voyeur* of lives you will never touch. How *could* they? It was a conspiracy, that's what it was. A Chinese torture. He could feel the weight of every fuck, drops of water pressing relentlessly against his forehead; but the pressure came from within, every drop desperate to escape and tap tap tapping lustfully towards the light.

Damn. Now he had a hard-on there was hardly any time to do anything about it. But waste not, wank not, he decided, and prepared his missile for take-off. This time the enemy would stand no chance. He tried to recall the theme tune of *Thunderbirds*, which seemed appropriate under the circumstances, and allowed his hand to conduct the movement in time with his humming. He also tried to summon up enthusiasm for his wife as she might appear on a good day, but found he couldn't remember the first thing about her face. Maybe if he started with her eyes, her blue eyes . . . No, surely they were

9

brown, to match her dark hair . . . But her hair was light . . .
He would let her go, let her go . . . Think of that Lady Penelope
instead. She'd been a bit of all right . . . sensuous, pink shining
lips . . . Was she *Thunderbirds* or *Stingray*? No, *Stingray* was the
one with the Page Three mermaid, Marina, who couldn't
speak, couldn't screw, but had all the plastic surgery pilots after
her tail, tide in, tide out. Who else? Who else? Quick, oh quick,
more women . . . Remember their faces, glassy eyes . . . The
Flintstones . . . No, no, shapely women but tight-arsed as hell,
you can always tell the type . . . Bill and Ben and the cock-
teasing Weed . . . no, you can't screw a weed . . . But Lady
Penelope, oh, Lady Penelope . . . Money, good looks, gorgeous
pink car, thick lips, God, he could chew that mouth, feel that
blonde hair wrapped around his fingers . . . expensive clothes
. . . under her furs, tits of pure plastic . . . the money, those legs
. . . those legs she kept so well hidden under her skirts . . . feel
her thighs . . . the money, the . . . oh, Lady Penelope . . . oh,
Penelope, Penny, Penny . . . doll . . . Oh, doll . . . There. At
last. It wasn't the Niagara Falls, but these days he had to be
grateful for small mercies. God, had he sunk to this? Turned on
by the thought of a plastic doll? Lord. What on earth had
possessed him to think he'd get away with it with Lady Penny?
There'd have been that Parker to contend with first. Her
Ladyship's snotty-nosed chauffeur whose nasal defect had
shown no sign of improvement in all the years he'd worked for
her. You'd think she'd have lashed out on a bit of private
surgery, given his dedicated service, wouldn't you? These
women with money were all the same. No, he was well out of
that one. He'd stay away from women like that Lady Wash-
your-prick-before-you-touch-me Penelope.

Salmon remained beside the toilet bowl, watching his semen
curdle in the blue water, one of the many little Mediterranean
effects with which his wife had characterized their bathroom.
He was glad to have discoloured it. She was so fussy about the
toilet, he had given to wanking into paper tissues. It wasn't
simply their absorption properties he relied on; they also
soundproofed his activity and, as the years went on, he was
certain the process was becoming much noisier than ever it had
been in his youth. Now, he could almost hear his penis creaking
with each movement like the regular swinging of a door in

10

desperate need of oil. It was as if his organ had decided to create a life of its own, outside his control; his Frankenstein's monster, which would one day rise up and walk away of its own accord.

The nightmares relating to his organ's other-worldliness had been the first sign that something was wrong. They had started on his fiftieth birthday. The first dream took him back to Norwich and the small terraced house where he grew up. He was sitting on the lawn in the back garden of his house. It was a fine day and there was no wind. He watched his mother leave the house by the back door; she was carrying an enormous yellow bucket which she brought over and placed beside him. The bucket was filled with soapy water and he helped his mother wash his father's socks. But no matter how hard he scrubbed and rinsed, scrubbed and rinsed again, they still gave out more dirt. Eventually he gave up trying, took the socks to the washing line and pegged them up to dry. When he had finished, he stood back to look at the row of dripping socks and saw that they had turned into penises: all exactly the same shape and colour, and each one his own. He had to get the line up into the air before . . . before what? But regardless of how hard and fast he turned the rusty handle on the post, the line would not lift the penises. The dream had ended when he was woken by the sound of his own voice shouting 'Down, boy! Down!' – presumably to the family spaniel whose greatest delight had always been in stealing clothes from the line and attacking them with psychopathic verve.

More recently, there was the dream in which his penis grew, just like Pinocchio's nose, every time he told a lie. As lying was an essential part of the teaching profession, the great snake took no time at all in achieving quite remarkable feats of longitude. No matter how many different and ingenious ways he found to wrap it about his person, still it defeated him and found ways to ridicule him in front of his colleagues and pupils: in morning assemblies; at staff meetings; and in County Hall, where it left, in its wake, a long, crawling tail of luminous semen.

The dream had made him increasingly self-conscious. He could feel them when he woke, wrapping him like a cobweb, and no amount of clawing would tug them free. The horror would stay with him throughout the day, when, at work, his

11

hand would suddenly reach for his crotch as though remembering, too late, that it had forgotten to zip up his fly.

He swopped his black underpants for a pair of red and stretched the waist elastic until it returned to his belly with a slap, reminding him of fifty years' accumulation of fat. But maybe it wasn't so very much after all. It was amazing what a few sperm could do for the ego, regardless of the size of your aquarium. Even if he was overweight, it couldn't have been more than a few pounds. Men could get away with it, anyway. He was just a bit older, that's all, and, at half a century, more than a little resentful at his wife's ability to enjoy jigsaws more than sex.

Josephine's idea of eroticism was the completion of a three-thousand-piece puzzle. Even on their honeymoon, she had managed to finish two Rembrandt scenes, two portraits of the Queen Mother and a puzzle of the BBC 2 testcard. Jigsaws were the only 100% proof contraceptives around. 'Coming to bed?' he sometimes managed to ask her, in moments of reckless enthusiasm. 'Sorry. Have to finish this cloud/coronet/wagon', or whatever other senseless piece of the thing it was. Just to spite her, he put on a yellow shirt of which she had a particular loathing and went down to breakfast.

Salmon removed the knitted egg-jacket (what was it? A jumper? Skirt? Waistcoat?) from the hard-boiled egg Josephine had left in the fridge. Why had she recently taken to dressing everything up? Hats, scarves and socks were finding their way onto the most unlikely of objects. The air freshener in the bathroom was now a crocheted swan; even the toilet rolls had a bigger wardrobe than he. Yesterday, it had been the cutlery. He found it tightly packed, in groups of six, in white, rib-stitch condoms, lining the drawers like the penial souls of lovers dead and gone. Perhaps he, too, would be made to wear the woolly sheaths during the cold winter nights, his balls snugly wrapped in adjoining egg-jackets. He pulled viciously at a loose thread in his designer breakfast: it unravelled several more stitches to create a balaclava. He was pleased with the effect and re-set it over the shell for a first fitting. It was as unbecoming as the crinolines left by his wife for the milkman to fit obscenely over each bottle. Salmon noticed that in school, too, superfluous dress was now the rage: gloves without fingers (if it was cold,

12

why exclude fingers from warmth? If it was not cold, why wear gloves?); ankle-warmers on a hot July afternoon. He removed the balaclava and tapped the egg sharply against the edge of the kitchen table. The shell crushed and formed a dent; a fine, smiling crack appeared around the middle. With quick, pecking motions, his fingers removed the tiny fragments, along with their rubbery undercoat, from the smooth, bald flesh that revealed itself underneath. He took sadistic pleasure in peeling away the large pieces: slowly and carefully, listening for the suck that was like a kiss being pulled apart. Picking at his sunburn had always given him the same pleasure: not the small white pieces (they were no better than glorified dandruff), but the large swollen pads of fine, rice-paper skin. When the blister broke, he could lift it at the edge and pull a whole continent away.

But the ultimate pleasure was a chocolate marshmallow: crushing the chocolate and eating the jigsaw a piece at a time. Sucking the mallow from its base in one soft lump; the final nibbling around the circumference of the biscuit. It was impossible to stop at one. The box of mallows looked un-balanced with a single space; a balance that could not be regained until the box was once again empty. So although he gained perfect satisfaction from his personal hatching of a hard-boiled egg, he could not dissociate the experience from that of mallow sickness. Neither could he suck on a mallow without feeling remorse for the blob of jam which remained on the biscuit. If the heart of his hard-boiled egg was a yellow, aborted chick, then the single red eye seemed also a drop of life, more blood shed for man's appetite.

The Main Stable

Riverside Comprehensive School was christened in September 1971, the first year of 'official' comprehensive education. Previously the County Grammar School for Boys, it therefore followed quite naturally that it now be considered the more desirable establishment of the new order for the Endridge County region. Its catchment area included most of the west side of the river, although several bus loads were driven in daily

13

from the docks, twenty per cent of them black, so that a greater variety of breed and colour might give justification to the term 'comprehensive'. Orphans, blacks, Asians – every good comp. should have a few. If there was a limp or a glass eye among them, all the better. The headmaster was able to say, therefore, with all honesty, that Riverside (unlike its middle-class rival, Alderstoke) was a genuine product of the new system. Dr J. P. Edwards M.Sc. sent his green and white striped booklet to the parents of Form One, as they signed up their loved ones to be guinea pigs under the new regime. Headmaster of the Boy's Grammar School prior to the changeover, he now realised that it was his duty to update the old understanding of 'education' for the benefit of the modern age. Following a close reading of Marx, Shakespeare and John Stuart Mill over a period of several days, he finally came up with a suitable definition. A school should be based upon certain principles, namely those of education, from the Latin *educo*, meaning 'I lead out'. This involves a drawing upon the individual's strengths and should operate not solely to *put in* knowledge. A school must be 'a community in which the individual is valued in his (or her) uniqueness and respected for himself (or herself); a member therefore contributes his (or her) qualities to the community as a whole'.

The introduction to the first comprehensive school booklet took the doctor three weeks to prepare. Intense and passionate, the rhetoric burrowed through many tunnels of verbosity before reaching its peroration: 'We aim to provide an education that proffers to the individual (and we at Riverside *stress* individuality) opportunities to develop, expand and sustain a sense of vocation . . .' (alas, a printing error brought attention to the individual's 'sense of vacation') '. . . in order that he (or she) might achieve self-fulfilment: both in the context of his (or her) awareness of society and the world at large; at all times recognizing the value of hard work, self-discipline, respect and altruistic concern for all others at all times and in all circumstances, regardless of colour, creed or limb deficiency.'

Dr Edwards decided to retire within one year of serving the new system. Six months later, it was decided for him that he end his service with life. His wife donated all his books to the school and presented a trophy to be awarded annually on

14

Speech Day: The J. P. Edwards Memorial Perseverance Prize. It came to be known as the cup for the most consistent failure.

Kenneth Salmon inherited a split school: the traditionalists versus the modernists on the staff – those who believed in the old methods and insisted on wearing their graduation gowns at all times, and those who stuck to creativity and psycho-analytic persuasion – and between the secondary moderns and ex-grammars among pupils. The former found themselves demoted three forms from 'A' to 'D', to accommodate the new intake, and the latter suddenly found themselves grouped with Eleven Plus rejects for sport and smaller language classes, when the sec. mods. took this opportunity for revenge and tyrannized their opponents. It took Salmon six years to develop what he called a comprehensive school, when that first intake left at the end of Form Six. 'Streaming' became an old-fashioned word in favour of 'sets', and Form One was awarded the privilege of having mixed abilities working in the same room.

Salmon had been head of Riverside for eleven years. During that time, he had seen it grow to a population of twelve hundred pupils and seventy staff. This morning, September 5 1983, he stood at the window of his study trying, once again, to recognize faces among the children entering the grounds. Not much chance of that; he didn't even recognize the staff. The children were certainly growing smaller every year; or maybe, because of financial stringency, their parents were buying them bigger Burberrys and duffle-coats. This year, the new intake had created seven classes in Form One, and suddenly, Salmon felt that the years were moving closer together, faster. Now he felt as if he were working a conveyor-belt, at the end of which he would file the contents into IN and OUT trays. He left the window, opened his cabinet and flicked through the newly organized Speeches, Prayers and Admonitions section: 'A', Autumn; 'W', Welcome. He sat at his desk and rehearsed the morning's introductions for both staff and pupils. He was always slightly nervous. It stemmed from an early experience at Sunday School. He had been cajoled into reciting a poem one year at the Harvest Festival. Thick clusters of purple hydrangeas curved along the arch above his head in the pulpit;

15

he kept his eyes fixed on the golden sheaf of bread on the table and began:

> The cold wind doth blow
> And we shall have snow,
> And what will the robin do then
> Poor thing!

Everyone laughed. Each time he said 'Poor thing!' they did the same. His mother had tried to convince him that they liked the way he said it; he was earnest, sincere. But he had never been able to escape the fear that people were laughing at him. As a headmaster, of course, they invariably were. As a pupil, he had laughed at his teachers; as a teacher, he had laughed at the heads; as a headmaster, he could only listen to the laughter of others. He returned to the window in time to see his deputy park his bicycle in the sheds.

Stables and Fittings

> *A horse is naturally inquisitive by nature, and for this reason should be provided with a loose-box, which allows for greater movement. Overcrowding in stables should always be avoided; lack of space induces boredom, and often, as a result, bad habits such as crib-biting and wind-sucking. Also common in cramped conditions is the problem of 'casting', when the horse is unable to rise, once down.*
> *Horses should be allowed to see each other, although the possibility of their being within easy biting distance must be avoided. Windows, fastenings, light fittings, electrical supplies and other gadgets should also be kept well out of reach. To reduce the risk of colds and ailments, a constant supply of fresh air is essential.*

The Start of the Season

BIRTHS
Starlight Express and Count Tolstoy on 20 August, an Arab: Ruby's Way.

16

MATINGS
Holding Forth with Blake's Seven (née Blake's Six) on 29 July.

DEATHS
Moonshine, on 21 August, aged 14 years, after a long bout of fetlock gangrene.

King of the Orient, 28 July. Passed peacefully away in a manger.

INTRODUCTORY MEETING FOR STAFF
MONDAY 5 SEPTEMBER 1983
MEMORANDUM

'Rees, Frank, after a long illness . . .' The headmaster was coming to the end of the start-of-term Important Notices.

Graystone placed a tentative hand on Salmon's arm and whispered in his ear. The head felt relieved that the atmosphere had been broken. He hated this first staff meeting of the term; he felt so exposed, as if he personally were responsible for the information he conveyed.

'Oh . . . er . . . Harold's just informed me that . . . er Frank isn't dead . . . I . . . er . . . must have misunderstood . . . er . . .'

'Just looks it, eh!'

'Been dead for years if you ask me!'

Salmon tried to regain composure. 'You'll be pleased to know that John Halliday of last year's Upper Sixth won £200 for the school and £100 for himself in the Aubrey's Art Competition.'

'He ought to have. He did bugger all else for two years,' said David Anderson.

Peter Allen glowered. 'The reason he so wisely dropped the tedium of Maths "A" Level was because he happened to be exceptionally talented.'

'I'd be talented if I had the time.'

'Welcome to Mr Lissold who's joined the Geography department . . .'

'Hard luck.'

'. . . and Miss Lyle, who'll be bringing a little intellectual spunk into the History department with her PhD on Henry

17

VIII's ... er ... seventh wife. Also, welcome to Mrs Harris –
it's always pleasing to see a lady with an aptitude for
Mathematics – and Miss Sykes, a physicist who'll be helping
out in the R.E. department.

'A quick rundown on the morning then ... The bell will go
in five minutes and we'll have everyone in the hall for
Assembly. After we've sorted out our forms, we'll take them
away to our respective rooms. The first two lessons before break
will be form periods; the next three, normal classes, except for
Form One who will stay with their form tutors until lunch-time,
and Form Six who will stay with theirs until third lesson
when ...'

'Uh ... Mr Salmon ...' Roy Dixon, the Academic
Registrar, looked up from an enormous white card on which he
had been manoeuvring square stickers of every imaginable
colour. He looked up like a child, baffled by the rules of a new
game. '... No ... uh ... what I thought we'd do was ... yes
... now let me see ... yes, got it. The first two lessons will be
form periods for all forms, apart from those who won't yet have
been placed because of their subject combination, and they'll
go to room four where Miss Lamb's form usually is and *they* will
have to go to the hall for those two lessons; then the next three
will be normal lessons for all except Form One ...'

'That's what I said.'

'Yes ... right ... but if Form One are in their form rooms,
the classes having lessons will have to follow the alternative
timetable until lunch-time, and the teachers who would
normally be taking lessons but are tied up with Form One will
have to be covered by teachers on the alternative staff list. I also
think that now, Form Six will not be able to go to their form
rooms *until* third lesson, because Alex and John will be sorting
out problems that might occur as a result of the form periods
with the Lower and Middle parts of the school.'

'I don't really see how that affects the Sixth Form.'

'Well, Alex wanted to have the Sixth Form to help out a bit;
show the first years around.'

Brian Cottrill joined in. 'I don't see why the teachers of each
form can't do that. The Upper School has to be our priority. I
want to get the Sixth Form sorted out before break. There are

18

bound to be the usual clashes of subject; we'll spend the rest of the day sorting those out.'

'The only reason there are clashes,' said Dixon, 'is because pupils are suddenly allowed, without anyone informing me, to do obscure combinations.'

'Ah, the joys of comprehensive thought,' said Graystone.

'I must say,' intervened Salmon, 'I'm not happy about leaving Form Six to wander the corridors aimlessly. Alex, do you think you could manage without them?'

'Sure. We'll use the teachers.'

'Well, mine will be staying in the classroom,' said Esther Lamb. 'P.E. is by far the most demanding part of the curriculum. I do enough running about as it is, I don't want to be traipsing round with my form all day as well. It just isn't practical to have two hundred children cavorting in the school grounds. They might damage the running track.'

'Alex, do you really think it's necessary to take them outside? Couldn't the teachers draw maps on the blackboards?'

'Sure. We'll use the blackboards.'

'Good. Well then . . . First two lessons, form periods for all, apart from those without forms. Third, fourth and fifth, form periods for Form One, indoors; normal classes for everyone else. Normal rooms for Form One, alternative rooms and alternative teachers for a small percentage of others. Now has everybody got that?' Salmon paused like a vicar conducting a marriage service, waiting for objections to the coupling of two seemingly simple ideas: Man and Woman. He let them hang in the air, awaiting assassination. 'Right. Thank you. A very happy term to you all.'

Dixon sighed and began to pull apart his mosaic, each sticker representing a person, place or time, though his plans had not in the least been affected. When the new kaleidoscope was complete, he sighed, smiled and retired to his enclosure.

'Sir, Mr Powell told me to come and see you. I've got a clash between Economics and German on Wednesday afternoons.' A tall, dark-haired boy peered down into the frustrated eyes of the Registrar.

'And I've got four between Biology and English,' piped up a girl, second in the long queue.

19

'Biology and English! But that's Arts *and* Sciences. Can't you stick to one or the other? Who's your form teacher?'

'Mr Hayward, sir.'

'Well, have a chat with him about dropping English.' Dixon suddenly remembered that Hayward was head of English. 'No, Biology. Right, what's your problem?' He moved along the line, trying to persuade pupils to see the error of their choices. When he reached the end, the disquieting noises of the wild appeared to have been successfully subdued. Dixon tucked his clipboard under one arm, and with the other attempted to usher pupils back through the doorway.

But this year's stable refused to be so easily broken. Dixon's whipping gestures merely excited them further and a united braying of discontent burst from the disgruntled parade.

'But my father says I must do French or I won't get a job abroad.'

'But I want to go to Cambridge and I haven't got a language.'

'But I like English.'

'I haven't got an 'O' Level in it.'

'I don't like the teacher.'

'I want to do Russian 'A' Level.'

'I didn't want to come back anyway.'

By break, Roy Dixon was once more buried amongst his papers. His winter hibernation had begun. It was fortunate he was such a competent administrator, he thought, or the school would be in absolute chaos.

The Foal Enters the Stable

Timothy Leach listened for his name and then followed, with thirty others, the head of Andrew Young, up the stairs to room twelve.

Young's register reflected the more artistic side of his nature. He enjoyed these first meetings with new classes at the beginning of term when he would meticulously, like the pupils he taught, ink in the first markings on clean white pages.

'Good morning, 1T.'

'Good morning, Sir.' A few children rose, hovered and sat again.

'When a teacher comes into a classroom, 1T, you should remain standing until you are informed to do otherwise. Please remember that for the future.' Everyone stood. 'Right . . . *do* sit down, Form One . . . Now, my name is Mr Young and I will be your form teacher for this year. I'll also be taking you for History. The first thing I want to do is take your names.' He opened the large grey ledger on his desk and took a pen from his briefcase. The class was silent.

'Right. Does anyone have a surname beginning with the letter "A"? Boys first.' A boy with ginger hair, seated at the back, raised his hand.

Young worked through the boys' surnames in block capitals of blue-black ink, seating them against the margin, followed by a comma and a more elaborately detailed Christian name. He finished 'Osmond' and looked up again.

' "P" – does anyone's surname start with the letter "P"?' A hand went up halfway along the third row. 'Name, please?' Young held his pen poised above the page, as if about to sign a treaty of international significance.

'Timuffy, sir.'

'Timothy what?' Young took special pains to articulate the correct pronunciation and made a note for the English department's attention.

'Timuffy Leach, sir.'

'LEACH!'

'Ye – es, sir.'

'But that's an "L"! We're now on "P", lad. Have you been asleep?'

'No, sir, I . . . I just couldn't follow. You went too fast.'

Young started at the accusation. He took an instant dislike to the little Leach, framed behind his National Health spectacles.

'Too fast! You're in secondary school now, you know. This is where you learn to be more efficient, more quickly, Mr Leach.' He looked down the list of names on the register – Jones, Martin, Merran, Neally, Osmond. 'But Leach is four names ago!' Young gasped at the extent of the operation he would have to perform on the new page. He felt the dismay of a child making his first blot of the term in a new exercise book. 'Come

21

here, Leach.' Timothy tried to move inconspicuously forward. It seemed hours before he reached the accusing stare of the master. 'I want you to go down to the office and ask for some liquid paper – do you understand?' He addressed Timothy as if it were his first visit to the planet.

'Y . . . You . . . can borrow mine if you like, Sir.'

Young softened. 'Thank you, Timothy. Good lad. Shows you have a concern for neatness . . . well, run along then.'

Timothy, blushing, returned to his seat and then to the teacher's desk, on which he placed the small bottle, a golden apple. Young dabbed at the page, an artist administering the final touches to a great painting.

'It's a school rule, incidentally, that liquid paper must not, under any circumstances, be brought on to school premises. I'd better hang on to this, Timothy. You can collect it from me at the end of the day. Sit down, please.'

Young finished filling in the class names, blew on the final touches of wet ink and closed the book. The door opened. The Head came in with another boy.

'New boy for you, Mr Young. Got a bit lost on his way. Thank you.'

Young re-opened the register. 'Name, please?'

'Stephen Campbell, Sir.'

The First Fence

'One down, three hundred to go,' said Ken Salmon to himself. The twenty to four bell had rung. He watched the chaotic streams of children fighting for the main door.

'Walk!' shouted Miss Calne. Her commands echoed hoarsely in the corridor. 'Where's your blazer! . . . Don't give me that look, young lady!'

She really cares, thought Salmon. About all the wrong things.

CHAPTER TWO

ON THE CIRCUIT : ESTABLISHING
A ROUTINE

A regular routine is essential for horses, and thought must always be spared for the animal's well-being and comfort. Adjustments may be made to the basic framework of the routine, provided that feeds are kept small and regular, and exercise is permitted at least two hours a day. It must also be remembered that horses need adequate rest.

It was Salmon's twenty-first hard-boiled egg of the term. His twenty-first perfect egg; the start of the fifth week of the academic year. As long as the perfect eggs continued to hatch, Riverside would run smoothly. At weekends, he avoided eggs, so that the two day break would not be spent in anticipation of the following week, should a rubber undercoat prove stubborn or a bad yolk appear. But it was four weeks into term and the shells were still peeling beautifully; the solid whites opening with the ease of ripe horse-chestnut cases; the yolks set firm, and clean as conkers.

The twenty-first hard-boiled egg, however, turned out to be not hard-boiled at all. As Salmon pulled the last piece of shell away, a fissure appeared in the flesh and a golden tear escaped. He sighed. Still, he had had a good four weeks.

Eggs had played a significant part in the development of Salmon's career. Early on in life, his interests in Physics had been awakened by an experiment he learned in junior school: pressure is applied to an egg at each of the rounded ends, and however intense the squeezing between fingers and thumb, the shell will not break. What had particularly interested him was

23

the fact that he failed. Constantly. For some reason, when his voice broke he was able to master the trick and he advanced to greater complexities: directing eggs into glasses of water, albumen juggling that seemed to go against the force of gravity. Again, success proved elusive for many years to come.

But despite failure, Salmon recognized something in those early tricks: the quality of magic. His lack of understanding of cause and effect only added to his enjoyment. It was not necessary to know How and Why; only When; the effect, without the cause. Many years later, when he was considering becoming a teacher, it was that same desire to present unexplained phenomena that helped him make up his mind. He pictured himself at the front of a class – his audience – performing tricks of a seemingly supernatural kind. He wanted to give them illusions. There would be no Method, Result and Conclusion to record in an exercise book. They would remember only the moment. When. Magic.

The years following the experiments with eggs saw an enlarged repertoire: balloons sticking to walls; hair raised with brushes – including that of Chan, his Persian cat, vigorously brushed hundreds of times a day in order to make sparks leap from his poor, bristle-birched body. Chan was always a willing victim, however, knowing that participation in such experiments brought a reward of fresh fish. He finally sacrificed himself in a thunderstorm, when the young and eager-to-learn Kenneth (for whom the word of Benjamin Franklin was not word enough) wished to prove it for himself that lightning was an electrical phenomenon. He took his Red Devil kite to the nearest hill in the hope of collecting electricity. He threaded a key on the end of the wet string and waited for electricity to create sparks. Sadly, the Red Devil lost its essential horns at a height of three feet; Chan caught pneumonia and was taken the same distance in the other direction; and the fourteen-year-old Kenneth went back to rubbing balloons.

Salmon's early interest in the phenomenon of electricity was intensified by a certain kinship he felt with Thomas Edison, initially through sympathy with the six-year-old inventor whose father had publicly beaten him for his stupidity. Salmon remembered many such beatings from his own father. In Edison's continued failure to cultivate popularity and his

24

eventual walking out of school (having been told his brain was 'addled'), he recognized something of himself. He saw each of them as a 'negative' force – capable of existing freely and alone; a rare ability. While all around, the rest of society was forced to operate as 'positive': having to exist in close conjunction with other people, other places, other things; able to operate alone for only brief periods. A 'negative' existence was, therefore, the more positive one: one that did not operate by the standards of others. And somewhere along the line, the two spirits of Thomas Edison and Kenneth Salmon, two freely floating negative bodies, linked up and became a single positive force.

It would have come as a humiliating shock to Kenneth, when pronouncing to the world 'I'm going to be an inventor', to have been patted on the head and told that his destiny was to teach: to be cast for eternity into the very institution he longed so hard to be rid of. Now he could not recall where the currents, somewhere along the line, had crossed, and his future been re-circuited. The only connection he could make was when, in moments of regression into the past, asking himself 'Why am I doing this?' he came up with the answer that education was like an electric charge.

That was what he had told them at his interview for teacher-training. They'd liked that. After weeks of hearing 'I want to communicate with people', it was hardly surprising.

'A fluid,' he had said, '– that is, the teacher – passes into a body – the pupil – in order to change it.'

Hm. Good. Very good.

'But of course, I don't see teaching just as a means of passing on knowledge . . .' The analogy started to make increasing sense.

Oh?

'You see, the basis of two distinct electric fluids is that they're both equally mobile and both existent together in equal amounts . . .'

Yes, yes. Thank you. Good morning.

The twenty-first breakfast egg of the term continued to pour onto the plate: through the hillock of salt and into the white bread triangles. Salmon pushed the plate aside and went in search of his briefcase.

'I'm off now,' he called upstairs. A bed creaked and there was a grunt from his wife. An alarm clock awoke with a long burp.

Morning Timetable

7.00 a.m.	*Refill water buckets*
	Supply horses with hay
	Muck out
	Quarter
7.30 a.m.	*Feed*
9.00 a.m.	*Remove droppings*
	Exercise
11.00 a.m	*Supply horses with water, if necessary*
	Give horses a small armful of hay, during washing
12.00 noon	*Remove droppings and feed*

If the next traffic-light is green as I approach it, I will live until the age of seventy. If I can overtake the blue car before the roundabout, I will have a good Christmas. If rain starts to fall before I reach the school gates, I will have chips for dinner.

Every morning, Kenneth Salmon gave significance to a new set of landmarks to add interest to the journey he made in his car to school. It was a route he had come to hate. Familiar objects met him at the same time in the same places, coming upon him slyly like inquisitive neighbours checking his movements. His young daughter, who had been working in the cinema during the summer holidays, had told him how she came to dread specific parts of each film. When Peter Pan loses his shadow, I know there's another hour to go, she had said. Salmon felt the same, but his calculations hurried him on too quickly to the destination. When I turn right at the top of the hill, I'm almost there. When I pass the 77 bus-stop on Weyberry Road, I have arrived.

Something happened to him when he passed the school gates. He felt it. Physically. It was like passing through a time barrier and automatically taking on the different character-istics of the new age. He could not remember precisely when he had first noticed the change; because it was something to which he could attach no name, he had not thought it significant. He accepted without question his change of skin and operated from within it for as long as the environment required. When he passed the school gates at the end of the day, he felt his spirit changing colour; his face itched as the muscles re-formed themselves; he felt his thoughts shuffle away to different corners of his mind.

The playing-fields. The swimming-pool. A dead bird in the middle of the road. A yellow plastic litter-bin melted on a lamp-post. The church clock. He checked his watch against the church clock. Every morning. Today he goes to do the same, but notices that the hands of the church clock have stopped at ten past five. He has also forgotten his watch. Which may or not have stopped at ten past five. He clicks his tongue like a second hand against the roof of his mouth. Tick. Tick. Tick. At the first stroke, on the corner of Weyberry Road, it will be 8.15 precisely.

Day twenty-one. He was dreading it. The egg oracle had prophesied the beginning of the end. How would it start, he wondered. Exams. There was always a row about exams at this time of year: the English department expostulating about the two sets of papers they would have to mark over the Christmas holidays; Art, Craft, and Home Economics departments insisting upon the necessity of about twenty hours of 'practicals' per child; Dixon flapping around with his instructions for alternative teachers in alternative rooms taking alternative pupils for alternative exams. Still, at least it kept him busy and well out of reach of education itself, while at the same time allowing him the illusion of being a real inmate.

Even more likely was the possibility that Harold would start the rot. So convinced was he that only out of chaos could order be born, that four weeks of seeming calm would, of necessity, have to be disrupted. First would be the headmaster-ing him with 'You-know-what-I-means' and obscure quotations. 'Headmaster, I have a young lad here who seems beset with the notion that he is Attila the Hun . . . "He who conquers others is strong", laddie, "He who conquers himself is mighty".' Poor Harold. He meant well.

What else could go wrong? Liz Caversham had started rehearsals for *Godspell*, scheduled as the Christmas production

27

'. . . I just can't direct while the cooks are banging their tureens . . .' Staff opposition would just about be ready for attack: 'I'm not letting kids out of my lessons for play practice. They're in school to pass exams.' 'But Art, Culture, the Soul'; 'O' Levels, 'A' Levels'; 'We can't wash the feet without Jesus'; 'Jesus hasn't done his homework'; 'He'll catch up, he's the Messiah'; 'He can go to hell.'

Every year produced the same problems; the form hardly changed. Salmon recalled how very different, during his early years as a teacher, each day had seemed; he had always been struck by the unpredictability of his life when he compared it to the more mundane existences of others. It was many years before he tired of his performance in the classroom, and when he did, it was less to do with himself, he supposed, than with what they called 'the changing of the times'. The tricks lost their magical quality as the audience seemed to adopt a more cynical attitude year by year. Suddenly he felt embarrassed when he went out to face them; rather like a comedian who goes on stage, picks up his microphone and says, 'Look, I know you won't find this funny, but . . .' Idealism gave way under the inevitability of failure. He reached out to his pupils with trepidation and they, with their horse's sense of human fear, recognised it and consequently punished him for it. First, he lost the power to touch; second, the desire. In the future, he would keep them far enough away not only to be out of his reach, but for him to be beyond theirs. Let them see through his tricks, he would not allow them to see through himself. He sat them high up in the gods, in rows of darkness, and removed their opera glasses.

In the end, it was 'the system' he blamed for the change in his feelings. He realised he was impotent: impotent to change the things he disliked in the teaching profession: the dependence upon the examination system, the emphasis on apparently ludicrous rules, regulations and routines. Its suspicion of magic. Now, he decided, he would work his way up to a position from which he would be able to administer change. In the meantime, he would carry on with the mechanical day-to-day requirements of living; function competently; do his job and produce the so desired examination results. He did not need to feel anger towards the routine when he knew that at any moment he could easily have broken it.

Now, on day twenty-one, he wished he had done just that: pressed the 'STOP' button when it was still within his power to obey its command. He knew it would have been easy. But by the time he was in a position to call for change, he could not put a stop to the regular ticking of his body. He responded with irritation and hatred towards his inability to break both the pattern of himself and his situation. There was only one way to keep the feelings under control: by feeding himself with more and more programmes, rules and regulations. And he hated himself for his dependence upon them; his inability to prevent the automatic changing of his skin; and he was frightened by the fact that it had become the skin in which he somehow needed to be. Stripped of it, at the end of the day, he was raw and exposed. Now, every part of him, body, soul and mind, listened for and responded only to the tick tick tick of his drugged heart.

' "Routine is the god of every social system",' said Graystone. It was his first public warning of the term – the victim, a pair of psychedelic socks. Now the term had really begun. Graystone felt extremely good. For weeks he had been scouring the lower regions for a pair of offending feet. Usually it took only a matter of days into a new term before he found them. This time, however, the purge on uniform at the end of the previous school year had made it appear at first as if the days of clothing deviancy were over. Graystone had felt more than a little sad. After all, children were supposed to break rules; his job was dependent upon the fact that they did. How could he try to make them conform if they didn't break the rules?

Black. Dark grey. Charcoal. The boys stuck to their dark socks. Snow white. Off white. Grey. The girls were also off to a fine start. There had been an almost invisible blue stripe down the sides of one pair, but Graystone decided to wait for a real scoop. *Now.* These socks had certainly been worth waiting for.

He first heard of their whereabouts through the senior mistress. She and Graystone habitually exchanged reports of pupils wearing unacceptable dress, according to each of their personal quirks. Grace's 'thing' was blazers. It was a school

29

rule that all pupils while on school premises should wear their blazers, whatever the temperature. The rule had been amended slightly when, during the summer term, two Fifth Form girls, in the 85 degree heat, came into school wearing their blazers and very little else. Further protest and increasing frustration regarding her inability to deal with every absentee blazer gave Grace the idea of bartering information with Graystone. She was very knowledgeable on the whereabouts of coloured socks, and he on the non-whereabouts of blazers. Rather than exchange jobs (which would have demanded a rather complex re-programming of their senses), they adopted an efficient system of espionage. Information was stored mentally, for fear of less competent prosecutors discovering written evidence and reaching the guilty party first. Although neither would admit it, each also kept a record of their number of exchanges. At present, Graystone was six blazer culprits in hand. Only when Grace described the socks – which, he had to admit, sounded particularly wayward – would he give her two names from his list.

Once a name changed hands, it was left to the recipient to uncover further information before setting out to trap and finally catch the culprit. However, no sooner had Graystone checked the boy's movements than he came upon the socks quite by accident. Now he felt cheated. If he would have found them anyway, it was hardly a fair exchange. These socks had walked up to him. Actually walked right up to the very spot where he had stationed himself for the mid-morning inspection.

'What's the time, Sir?' said the voice of the socks.

Graystone watched the lime spots dance on their pink background as the boy shifted his weight from one foot to the other.

'What are those!' he squeaked, shocked, yet also mesmerised by the luminosity before his eyes. ·

'What, Sir?'

'You're Andrew Hart, aren't you?' Graystone spoke as if he had found the missing link in a chain gang. He raised his eyes slowly to Hart's face. 'Where are your school socks?'

'Didn't wear them,' smirked Hart.

'I can see you didn't wear them – where are they?'

Silence.

'Ah, headmaster,' called Graystone, as Salmon attempted to sidle into his office. 'We have a young lad here who thinks he is Malvolio.'

Salmon caught 'olio' and noticed Graystone's anxious nodding towards the boy's feet. 'Has he seen the nurse?'

'Cross garters have nothing on these, headmaster,' said Graystone, ignoring the confusion. ' "Routine is the god of every social system" – Alfred North Whitehead, *Adventures in Ideas*, 1933. You'd do well to remember that, young man!'

'Yes, Sir.'

'Come and see me first thing tomorrow, wearing complete school uniform, or you shall have a taste of my . . . my . . .' He could think of no unpleasant enough concoction.

'Whitehead,' suggested Salmon.

'Of me,' substituted Graystone. That would have to do.

Footnote

Keeping up a good appearance is essential if a horse is to perform to the best of its ability. All animals must be thoroughly groomed each day and, when necessary, clipped. This will keep the skin clean and prevent diseases from spreading in what are inevitably dirty conditions.

Concerning a Rule: a Notice

'Concerning the bird hurt on Friday.'

Mr Graystone is pleased to announce that the boys who were present when the bird was injured came voluntarily to describe what happened.

The truth is, that the bird was not injured as a result of stone throwing. A seagull dived for a sandwich on the ground (sandwiches should not have been eaten outside anyway!); another bird also dived, landing on the first bird, whose wing was thereby damaged.

The inevitable result of stone-throwing – which is designed to hit someone – is that there will be a serious accident, or even death. NEVER throw stones again. If pupils had not eaten or

31

left food on the hockey pitch in the first place, none of this would have occurred.'

And isn't that a comforting thought,' said Salmon.

Entraining

> *One important aspect of the routine to regulate is that of bowel control. Specific times may be set aside for excretion and removal of droppings, though should a horse wish to dung when in motion, it is perfectly capable of doing so with ease.*
>
> *Unlike other herbivores, horses will not leave their dung anywhere. They may carefully smell out a spot where an acquaintance or family member has passed and dung in that same place. Passing dung is, however, infectious, and other horses will add to the heap. It is not uncommon, over a period of time, for several square yards to be covered.*
>
> *During dunging, the horse's head will be lowered, its ears turned back and the tail raised. The amount of dung passed depends upon the food eaten, breed, temperament and current state of mind. Nervous and frightened horses will dung if they are upset: for example, before a race.*
>
> *When a horse wishes to urinate, the intense expression on its face will indicate that the operation is in progress. The croup will be lowered, the tail raised and the hindlegs stretched apart. A horse will retain urine rather than wet itself by staling on hard ground. At all times, horses must be given the opportunity to stale in comfort.*

There was a knock at Salmon's door and before he could answer, his secretary entered the study.

'I'm afraid we've had a small mishap, Mr Salmon,' said Mrs Crashaw.

'It's about one of Mr Young's boys,' said Deirdre Fraser, Geography, manoeuvring herself around the secretary.

Mrs Crashaw stepped forward again. She felt it was her duty to act as middle-man between staff and the headmaster; the messenger whose task it is to soften the blow of undesirable news. On entering the office, staff were forced to perform movements akin to those in the game of Grandmother's Footsteps: step, stop, stand still as a statue; the object being to pass the secretary and reach Salmon's door before she did. Rarely were they successful. Despite Mrs Crashaw's sitting with her back to the outer door, the change in air pressure induced by a held breath meant that she became aware of the trespasser long before the inner sanctum could be reached.

'Timothy Leach – you know the Leaches, Headmaster?' said the secretary.

She had a preference for the instalment technique, and staff, if wishing to put their side of the story first, were forced to go for a quick summary of the plot before entering upon specifics.

'He's wet himself,' said Deirdre Fraser.

'On the floor,' said Mrs Crashaw.

'During my lesson.'

'Just before break.'

Salmon umpired the two stories before nodding a Thank-you-now-bugger-off to his secretary.

'Sit down, Deirdre. Now, what exactly happened?'

'Well . . . it's Timothy Leach. He said he . . .'

'What form is he in again?' Salmon poised, ready to take notes.

'1T, Mr Young's form. Anyway, just before break he asked if he could . . .'

'That would be second lesson . . .'

'Yes. Yes.' Really. The finer points were hardly relevant. 'And he asked if he could go to the toilet. I said that he couldn't and he would have to wait until break. He said that he was desperate and I . . .'

'Did he look desperate?'

'. . . ? . . .'

'Well, you know. Scrunched-up eyes. Contorted expression. That sort of thing.'

'Uh . . . yes, yes, I suppose he did have a sort of bunched-up look. Rather like a flower closing up for the night.' The teacher smiled, pleased with the analogy.

'A flower,' wrote Salmon. 'Then?'

'Well, then I told the class to stand, ready for the bell, and there . . . there was a puddle on the floor.'

'A large puddle?'

'Half puddle, half stream, I should say.'

'How would you describe the boy, generally speaking?'

33

'Quiet. No trouble. Gets on with his work.'

'Where is he now?'

'I sent him to the nurse.' All 'problems' which fell outside the basic categories of educational welfare always went to the nurse. 'I mean, I know I'm in the wrong . . . I mean, I know what it's like to want to go to the toilet when you can't – which reminds me, I'm pregnant again and am applying for leave next term – so it's not as if I don't understand . . .'

'It's all right. Now don't upset yourself. Here, have a fruit gum.' Mrs Fraser's tearful, mounting hysteria was somewhat appeased by the sweet. 'Now just go and wash your face in there . . .' Salmon indicated his private washroom. 'You can use the towel, I've only dried my hands on it,' he called after her. 'There was a young boy called Leach/Who went for a walk on the beach' he added to his notes – and crossed it out again. He saw Mrs Fraser to the door.

'Mrs Crashaw – would you find out when Mr Young is free and ask him to come and see me, please? Thank you.'

And they've gone again. He has shut them out. Now, only silence, but for the hurried nibble of typewriter keys in the office.

He had come to resent intrusion on his territory: both human interruption and the way that daylight forced him to acknowledge his surroundings. He hated the sun that now crept into the corner of his study, reminding him that the school day was not yet half over. He pulled down the blind and drew his curtains. The room took on the strange smell of semi-darkness he remembered from the sick room of his own secondary school; the suddenly distinct pattern in the curtains made him think of his old bedroom where as a child he had lain awake on summer nights; watched the shapes slowly dissolve as darkness shadowed them from the other side. His study took on a new dimension; outlines blurred, as straightness gave way to loosely hung proportions: cupboards, coping as if for the first time with their weight; walls forcing themselves to stand upright. And inside himself, too, Salmon felt the collapsing of his perfectly structured organs: the pain of something being dragged involuntarily down, along with the sagging room. He sat again, finally allowing himself to be drawn down with it. When he

34

closed his eyes, he felt the atmosphere close over him like a sulk. Now there was nothing but the pout of darkness to touch him.

He dreams of a black box. They have covered his eyes and placed a rope around his neck. Someone is pulling on the rope from in front; another pushes him from behind. He can sense the narrowness of air when he reaches the box; he recognises the smell of darkness. He hears strange noises and suddenly he knows that it is he who should be holding the rope, his hands guiding the reluctant creatures into the darkness. He tries to tell the body in front: no sound but that of a high-pitched whimper comes out. So he pulls on the rope, resisting the tug, and the noose tightens around his throat. He stamps his foot on the ground; there is only the rustle of the hay they have laid to silence his anger. He kicks against the ramps as the mouth of darkness starts to devour him. Every breath he takes sucks it closer around him; he is breathing his space away. He feels the walls of the box touching his body; soon, they are pressing against him. When they can move no closer, he tries to breathe again, but there is no air. No space. No light. His body squeezed to a capsule of darkness.

'Yes?' Mrs Crashaw rose quickly from her seat, made a sudden dash for the head's door and pressed her back against it.

'Is the Headmaster in?' asked Graystone. Suddenly he felt unable to attach a name to the elusive figure.

'He is.'

'Well . . .?'

'Perhaps it would be better if you came back another time.'

'*That*, Mrs Crashaw, is what you said yesterday, and the day before if I remember correctly. In fact, I have been trying since Monday morning to obtain an interview with the Headmaster and you have been making my task extremely difficult.'

'Well, I'm very sorry about that, Mr Graystone, but I really have been awfully busy. If staff brought their exam papers to me on time, maybe I could . . .'

'I'll wait.'

Mrs Crashaw bit her lip and resumed her typing. 'Very well.'

From Salmon's office came a low grating noise like that given off by a handsaw across a piece of wood. Tap tap tap. Small chipping noises followed.

'Ken! Ken!' called Graystone, like a Dr Who accomplice discovering the whereabouts of the master. The sawing stopped. 'I'd like to see you – just for a minute.' Silence. 'It's about the staff meeting this afternoon.' The sawing began again, once more picking up its regular rhythm. 'Will you be at the meeting?' Graystone attempted to shout above the noise.

'I told you,' said Mrs Crashaw, triumphant.

'What's he doing in there? . . . You know . . . I mean . . . People are beginning to talk.'

'It's not my place to ask,' said Mrs Crashaw, stiffening as Graystone took a step forward.

'I won't tell anyone,' whispered Graystone, 'you can trust me.' Mrs Crashaw looked doubtful. 'It'll be our secret.'

Mrs Crashaw relaxed. She checked the foyer, closed the office door and returned to her seat. She removed her glasses and leaned confidentially towards Graystone. 'To be honest, I haven't actually been inside since this . . .' (continued sawing, followed by a tap tap tap) '. . . started.'

'You mean, it's been going on for some time?'

'Only since Monday. Half past eight, Monday morning, in he comes carrying a huge cardboard box. "Don't disturb me today, Mrs Crashaw" – well, "Dorothy" was what he actually said – and in he goes. I haven't seen him since. He's in long before the rest of us in the morning and, as far as I know, leaves long after the rest of us at night.'

'Does he talk to you? You know, call out things?'

'Nothing. He comes out for his coffee, though – well, partly. He's about due for it now, actually. Just wait a minute.'

The secretary switched on the kettle. When it had boiled, she made a cup of black coffee and stirred in two sugars. She placed it on the floor the office side of Salmon's door. 'Just watch.'

Graystone watched. Mrs Crashaw watched. Steam rose from the cup as the loud gnawing continued. The bell rang for break. It was 10.40. The sawing stopped. A key turned in a lock. Mrs Crashaw pointed to the small but widening gap, as the door slowly opened. She and Graystone leaned forward, expectant fishermen poised over their floats. A dusty hand clawed its way

36

around the edge of the door. When it entered a hot cloud of steam, it lowered itself to grasp the cup. The coffee was picked up surreptitiously like a ransom and withdrawn inside.

'There!' said Mrs Crashaw with pride, as if she personally had engineered the whole operation.

'Is that it?' whispered Graystone. The secretary looked offended. 'I mean, doesn't it strike you as a . . . uh . . . a little odd?'

'Odd?'

'Well, yes. You know, I mean . . . it's not *normal*, is it?'

'He just wants to be left alone for a while, that's all.'

Mrs Crashaw adjusted her glasses and began typing once more. 'I'd feel exactly the same if I was in his position, being disturbed all day. He *is* the headmaster, after all. Why *should* he be pestered with school business?'

'I would very much like to know whether he intends coming to the staff meeting tonight. Could you ask him, please?'

Zzzzzz! Brrrrr! Graystone looked with alarm towards the door.

'It's all right. That means he's nearly finished. I'll ask him and give you an answer at lunch-time.'

Zzzzzz! Brrrrr!

'Thank you,' said Graystone, 'that would be much appreciated.'

Zzzzzz! Brrrrr! Tap tap tap. Silence.

CHAPTER THREE

JOCKEYS

JOCKEY: a man (orig, a boy) who rides in a horse race: a horse dealer: one who takes undue advantage in business.- v.t. to jostle by riding against: to manoeuvre: to trick by manoeuvring.- v.t. to seek advantage by manoeuvring.

There are several qualities to look for in a great jockey. He/she must:-

a) be temperamentally suited to the occasion of a big race

b) have the ability to 'read' a race accurately

c) be an excellent judge of pace and timing.

Stable Rationing

People enter teaching for many reasons, and if it was Salmon's relationship to eggs that determined his entry into the profession, it was Jonathan Hayward's relationship to his bladder that determined his. Teaching, it seems, is one of the rare professions that allows its members to go to the toilet, without appearing conspicuous, at any time, any number of times a day. During lessons, any excuse serves its purpose: I'm just going to get your books from the staff room; I'll just go and ask the Head about that . . . Hayward rarely had to leave his classes, however; the bells between lessons ensured that his bladder responded with Pavlovian instinct to the signal, allowing him to empty its contents during the convenient passage of time as he went from one classroom to another. If teaching is a vocation, it was Hayward's bladder that heard and responded to the calling long before the message reached his brain.

Now, on seeing Graystone take the chair for the staff meeting, Hayward wished with all his urinary tracts that he had emptied himself beforehand. At Riverside, any confrontation with Graystone meant confinement. In conversation, his words and dictionary of quotations weaved a tight net of verbosity around an unsuspecting victim. On entering a room, his overbearing physical presence released vibes that seemed to claw all space around himself, leaving the victim gasping for air. The very sight of him made Hayward's bladder ache for release. The man irritated him intensely; he felt the clenching of his insides when Graystone so much as entered his thoughts.

'I'm afraid that Ken has been called away to another meeting,' said Graystone, 'and he's asked me to take the chair.'

Hayward felt a sobbing in his crotch.

'Another meeting, my foot!' said Andrew Young.

'Lazy bugger!'

'Haven't seen him for days, come to think of it.'

'I thought he was dead.'

'Ladies and gentlemen . . . if we could commence, please. Number one on the Agenda, the school minibus . . . I'm afraid the minutes of our last meeting are delayed. Now, as you know, the last bus finally gave up the ghost on the Geography department's field-trip. You'll find in front of you a document in conjunction with the purchase of a new one that Mr Symms and his colleagues in the Geography department have drawn up . . .'

'There was a committee, actually.'

'Made up of your department,' said Malcolm Hewitt.

'Coincidence,' said Symms.

'Anyway, Mr Symms,' said Graystone, 'perhaps you'd like to say a bit about it.'

Staff looked despondently at the six-page document on the library tables around which they were seated.

'Yes, thanks. Well, as you see, it's not too lengthy,' said Symms, flicking through the six sheets in an attempt to minimise their bulk. 'I'd just like to invite comments upon the conclusions we drew. Perhaps we could start by discussing the advantages and disadvantages of purchasing a new bus. You see, the present bus is now totally beyond repair . . .'

'And whose fault is that?' A whisper.

39

'. . . So first, we have to decide if we really need a bus, and secondly, if so, where we will get the money to pay for it. A new fifteen-seater would cost in the region of £8,000. We might consider buying second-hand, but of course there's a high risk factor if we do that.'

'Do you think any expense of that sort can be justified?' asked Graystone.

'Of course!'

'Loaded question!'

'Unfair statement!'

'There are other questions we ought to ask first.'

'Quite right.'

'What about new curtains for the stage?' asked Liz Caversham.

'We need a new set of Bibles before that,' said Reverend Rock.

'And my D. H. Lawrences are wilting at the edges,' said Jonathan Hayward.

'I mean, what we really ought to be asking is whether the expense can be justified.'

'I suppose that brings us back to Harold's point.'

'Good point, Harold.'

'Very valid.'

'By far the most important consideration.'

'Carry on, Harold.'

'Yes, well, you know, I mean . . . I don't think we can spend this sort of money at the expense of other things. I mean, you know, if money had to come from the allowance I'm given for library books, then I would have to say no to a bus. I mean, it's books that are the foundation of the learning process and it's the education of the youngsters that should be our main concern.'

'That's all very well,' said Symms, 'but our department relies on a bus for field-trips and excursions, particularly with our new *Rocks Around the Clock* Geology programme.' Reverend Rock wriggled on his seat. 'They're a vital part of the education in the subject and we certainly wouldn't be able to provide such a good department without one.'

'That's a matter of opinion.' Another whisper.

'Remember *Operation Moondust* last term,' warned Graystone.

'I mean, you know, these field-trips don't always turn out to be . . . uh . . . educationally valid, do they?'

'If you're still referring to that Lesley Appleby business, I think it's too far gone to be relevant to us today.'

'No, no. Just making a small observation. I'm sure that the P.E. department would be just as grateful for a new bus.'

'You can't justify the expense for our sake,' said Hewitt. 'We take two teams most places and they can't even get into one.'

'I think we're discussing the possibilities of *one* bus at present,' said Graystone. 'Couldn't you consider taking one team one day and another the next? You know, I mean, when we're talking about saving money.'

'Well, I certainly couldn't give up two days instead of one,' said Esther Lamb.

'What exactly are you trying to say, Malcolm?' asked Liz Caversham.

'I just don't think you can accuse the P.E. department of taking £8,000 when a bus doesn't benefit us much anyway.'

'You go everywhere in it!'

'It's always out when other people want it.'

'Always muddy from football boots, too.'

'Lager cans hidden in the back.'

'My department never gets anything.'

'What about curtains for the stage?'

'Hymn books. Now there's something we really do need.'

'We've lost two cookers within a term.'

'I've got no decent paints.'

'You can't get to heaven in a bus.'

'Ladies and gentlemen!' Graystone held up his hand to still the noise. 'Can I ask you to consider, therefore, whether the expense of a new minibus can be justified. Maybe the old one is not *totally* beyond repair. But anyway, let's think about these issues and bring them to the next meeting. We don't have to go through everything in detail today. Next on the Agenda – litter – as a result, I am told, of there not being sufficient space for the sandwich-eaters to consume their lunch indoors. Now, when I was in room six I used to let the children use it as a sandwich room over the lunch hour. As we stopped classroom eating last year because of the mess, it now appears that we have a problem. Unless a member of staff is prepared to give up their room again, I can't see a solution.'

Patricia White, English, now stationed in room six, wanted no repeat performance of the stale crusts and peelings she had found stuffed into every available crevice.

'Well, I took pity on some this week,' said Liz Caversham, 'and let them use my room for half an hour.'

'Yes, well, as I said, when I was in room six I used to let them go in there . . .'

Then why the hell doesn't he let them go and masticate in his library, thought Patricia. Let them get their buttery finger-prints all over his books.

'I'm not making excuses,' said Hewitt, 'but often it's not the children who throw litter about. When I've been training kids after school and at weekends, I've seen starlings and blackbirds pulling rubbish out of the bins.'

'Strong birds,' said Graystone, imagining a starling with a yoghurt carton muzzling its beak.

'Couldn't we put some more tables out in front of the display cabinets?'

'I think Ken likes visitors to be able to see the school trophies when they're eating.'

'If the sandwich-eaters hurried down as soon as the bell went, they wouldn't have to wait for a free table.'

'Then we'd have long queues into dinner.'

'In front of the trophy cabinet.'

'Could we form two sandwich sittings?'

'Too much going on in the lunch hours.'

'Especially sport,' said Hewitt.

'The sandwich-eaters in my form say that the smell of school dinners puts them off their sandwiches.'

'I don't think sandwiches are at the root of the litter problem.'

'Neither do I.'

'Nor me.'

'We're trying to treat the symptoms, not the causes.'

'May I suggest,' said Graystone, 'that we ask the pupils for their ideas as to how we might improve the general appearance and overall tidiness of the school. For the class which comes up with the best suggestion, we'll allow them to purchase a small item with the reward.'

Yes. They would think over Graystone's suggestion. When they thought over the question of the minibus.

Jonathan Hayward listened to the voices that drifted further away as he became more conscious of the weight between his legs. Somehow he had to get away, though he knew he would be punished for doing so. Grace Calne, who worked out super-vision lists, kept careful note of staff misdemeanours; it became apparent who had sinned when staff found themselves repeatedly used for supervision in obscure parts of the school. To escape would be rudeness, thought Hayward; to excuse himself would draw attention to his leaving. He raised his hand.

'Uh . . . yes, Mr Hayward?' Graystone paused, and staff on all sides of the table turned their heads.

'Can I leave the room, please?'

'Uh . . . yes . . . yes, of course you may,' said Graystone.

'Thank you,' said Hayward, and left.

Kenneth Salmon listened at the keyhole of his door. Mrs Crashaw had packed up and left the office. 4.45. The staff meeting would now be in full progress. He longed for air and wanted to be free of the darkness of his box. It was growing cold and the early dark night cast a further blackness that he found frightening. Slowly, he turned the key and held his breath. There was no one in sight. In the distance, he heard the sound of an electric polisher moving closer. He listened to the whirring and humming of its brushes. He always felt a warm, tingling sensation throughout his body, when he heard some-one engaged in a physical activity around him while he remained inactive. He remembered being home from school, lying in bed ill, allowing the sound of his mother's movements to wash through him. She used to brush each stair, and as the brush moved upwards, he became conscious of the staircase as his own body; as if, with each brush-stroke, she were cleansing him, brushing the germs out from every corner of his flesh. She always brought the polishing into the bedroom; sat on the edge of his bed, bringing new life to dull silver and dusty ornaments.

43

He shivered as he watched her fingers probe the crannies of dirt in a silver fork, feeling the corresponding touch on a sensitive area of his own skin. It occurred to him that he had in fact undergone little change in the course of his life. Increasingly he could pinpoint the same thoughts and feelings he knew, quite clearly, he had experienced as a child. But now he remembered them with a sense of pain. He recalled his first holiday at the sea. All the main details of the trip he had forgotten – whether his sister had been there, too; where they had gone, even. What he remembered most clearly was his father, digging a hole in the sand. At first, the soft, warm sand resisted his touch: for every two handfuls he dug, one always fell back to its original place. Then, about a foot down, when it became wet and dark, he was able to scoop it, firm as ice-cream, into his palms. Watching his father's hands, the young Kenneth had suddenly felt the most unbearable sadness. And, as they travelled deeper, becoming smaller as the great mouth of the hole widened, he had wanted to cry. He would turn away and look directly into the sun, to find an excuse for his eyes filling up. Then he felt safe and able to turn his attention once more to the hole. Every so often his father would stop, brush the sand from his fingers and wipe the sweat from his forehead. Always, a few grains would leave their mark. And at the sight of that blemish on the smooth, sunburnt forehead as he bent down to recommence digging, the small boy could hold his tears no longer. He ran quickly to the sea, that he might taste the salt water and feel it, indistinguishable from tears, on his cheeks.

It was always with that sense of probing for detail that he now remembered his parents: his mother's small, rhythmical fingers working like a craftsman's tools; his father's square fingers fighting their way into small spaces. At that stage of his life he was working as a potter, and Salmon wondered if, when he sat his son on a wall at the beach and brushed sand from his feet, he handled him with the same thoughts as those with which he modelled his clay. Salmon remembered the spongy fingers' continuous travelling in the grooves until the grains of sand disappeared; the thumb set like a peg between the toes to keep them apart; his own small heels moulded dry by a clean palm. He never told his father that when, re-socked and shoed, they walked up the hill to the car-park, he felt the rattle of the sand that had remained trapped under his little toe. The cups, plates and bowls in the pottery also bore the same mark: slightly imperfect. And again, he had felt that he wanted to cry.

He remembered that he had tried to put a name to this feeling, angry that the adult world, oblivious to his suffering, could not be called upon to help him. To attempt an explanation, to try to pull whatever it was out from inside him and move it into the sun would have been, he knew, a violation of some sort of code. So he watched and waited, locked inside his own silence, until he was of an age when he himself could find it a name: examine each emotion by torchlight, under the bedclothes in the privacy of his own room; file it in a secret mental box, labelled, until meaning declared it safe.

But all these years later, it was as if he were still waiting; as if, in the morass of everyday life, he had nothing to cling to but these moments that were unable to articulate themselves. Last week he had been sitting opposite an old woman on the train. When the buffet opened, she went to buy a coffee which, on return, she placed carefully on the table. She appeared self-conscious and did not once raise her eyes to look around the carriage. Clearly an amateur when it came to British Rail fare, she slowly peeled back the foil seal on the tiny carton of milk. She jumped in shock as the liquid sprayed out, leaving a few drops on the back of her hand. Her cheeks reddened. Salmon could not say why, but the white spots staining the back of her wrinkled hand pained him; maybe, again, it was the hint of blemish that touched him. He turned away to look out of the window, where everything appeared neat, tidy, just like a picture book: trees, with green, cauliflower clouds of leaves; houses symmetrical; perfect pages, being flicked over in perfect rhythm. When he turned back, the woman's hand was clean once more. He managed to look her in the eye and offer a tentative smile that seemed, at one and the same time, both to offer, and beg, forgiveness.

Salmon opened his office door and listened more closely. The whisking sound of the polisher was approaching the end of the corridor. Soon it would turn the corner. If he was going to move, he would have to do so quickly. He could not be seen. What would they do if they caught him now? Throw the noose around his neck. Place the blindfold. Drag him, kicking and bucking, to the library. Tie him to a chair. Saddle him with questions. Demand answers to problems for which there are no solutions. If they took him now, they would stare at him accusingly, like a traitor they had discovered in their midst. They would treat him like the enemy. They would whip him into submission. They would want to know Why Why Why.

Purchasing Fittings and Accessories

Move droppings quickly and efficiently with DungDumper! Made from durable plastic (comes in brown or green), with pneumatic tyres and epoxy coated chassis. Special offer £45.99.

Ladies! Have you ever experienced soreness or discomfort in the saddle? Research shows that the classical posture which comes naturally to a man, is achieved by women only by their having to overcome essential physical differences. Gentle Touch is anatomically designed to ease tiredness and strain and to increase concentration. Call now on 08850 9312.

Top quality stables, tack rooms and feed barns. Cuprinol impregnated finish. Competitive prices.

'Thank you, ladies and gentlemen. That brings us to the final item on the agenda – a photocopier.'

It was now apparent why Graystone had wished to hold on to the possibility of £8,000 a little longer. An artful gleam came into his eyes as he raised the topic for which he had been waiting. He took an enormous sheaf of impressive brochures from his briefcase and handed them round.

'Let's start with an examination of the machine on page two,' he said, handing out the brochures. He waited for his class of teachers to find the right place. 'Grace – maybe you could read the piece about K106.'

Grace began. 'A convenient machine for all types of office. Economical to run . . .'

Several extracts were read. Graystone directed the reading around the table, ensuring that at least half of those present had a turn. The slower readers he allowed less time, lest the rest of the class might become bored and lose the thread of the story.

The merits of rival machines were debated as earnestly as those of prospective brides before an Indian arranged marriage. Sides were quickly and passionately taken; angry arguments and counter-arguments were exchanged. Would 'the machine' be a monster or a lamb? A demon or a god? How often would it be used? How much paper would it consume? Would it not constantly break down? Above all, *who would be in charge?* There was no easy resolution to the crisis: a vote would have to be taken.

'Please would all members of staff present, in favour of purchasing a photocopier from school funds, raise your right hand above your head,' said Graystone. His tone was more appropriate to that of a statesman addressing the U.S. Senate. As secretary of the staff room ways-and-means committee, he felt in serene control of the proceedings. A few tentative hands were raised. Frank Peters, Biology, saw Miss Lyle (a probationer) raise a little finger to hover cautiously – almost a vote – and felt a surge of manly compassion. Confidently he thrust his own plump fist into the air, smiled at her and watched with satisfaction as her tapering fingers mimed his own action. The English department was up in full force: James McGill lifted a hand of dirty finger-nails ('And he looked so smart at his interview,' Miss Calne had said); the long, sophisticated nails of Patricia White reflected the light as she raised her hand; Liz Caversham voted knowingly and her eyes squinted at her head of department who, with an empty bladder, sat smiling opposite. Hayward raised his hand.

The Geography department, a neat little threesome blocking the doorway like an archipelago in a river delta, held their right hands aloft, a we-never-get-anything-anyway expression on their faces: Geoff Symms, head of department; Philip Lissold, following suit, in order to increase his chances of promotion; and Deirdre Fraser, the pregnant map-reading expert.

Graystone's dark eyes, solid behind thick lenses, scanned the colourful arms, tiredly waving like drooping flags. Anxious to steal more votes to endorse his own opinion, he counted again, and recounted. When he was satisfied with the number, he jotted it down on his pad and continued.

'Thank you, ladies and gentlemen. I am most grateful for your careful consideration of the problem before us this afternoon. And now may we have the votes from those of you wishing to oppose the introduction of a photocopier.' He lowered his voice, as if the very thought of a negative response filled him with loathing. Two hands soared up before Graystone's voice had time to echo. He sighed. His tongue clicked nervously against his new set of teeth. This was what he had been dreading. The hands belonged to Malcolm Hewitt and Esther Lamb: what did a Games department want with a photocopier? It was ridiculous even to contemplate spending such an amount with the athletics equipment in such a state. Graystone tutted.

'But for those of us who never get to use the minibus because of sporting-trips, a photocopier would be very useful,' said Liz Caversham. 'And anyway, we need new curtains for the stage before we replace the athletics equipment – again.'

'I vote we think of buying a new minibus before anything else,' added Hewitt.

'Well, of course, you've worn the other one out,' said Liz.

'Please, please,' pleaded Graystone, 'we have already discussed the minibus. We are now on item three of the Agenda. Now can we please get back to the matter in hand.'

'Hmph!'

'All those against the photocopier . . . Hm . . .' Graystone tutted as other hands rose. Staff now began to contemplate how they too might lose out in other ways, should the machine come into being. The Language department remained split, as it did on most matters: the Belgian-born Katarina Ekkart now raised her hand in opposition to Julia Soames, a thirteen-stone French specialist. Katy (as Katarina was called) voted with Richard Smith (Dick, as Katy called him), and they exchanged smiling glances.

From some unknown source, the minutes of the last meeting appeared on the table.

'Now if we had our own photocopier, we would not have to rely on that belonging to the office and we would have had these minutes at the start of the meeting. But I mean, you know . . . one never knows when it might be useful . . .' Graystone tailed off. He took a final count of hands, hoping that at the

48

interruption some would have been lowered to rest. Now he caught them unawares and was sure that there were at least two less than at the first count.

'Thank you, ladies and gentlemen,' announced the Master of Ceremonies, 'the final result is as follows: twenty-seven votes in favour of the machine and . . . I'm afraid, the same number against. The result is unanimously even,' he chuckled. Then he remembered the seriousness of the situation. 'Well, what do we do now?'

'If Jenny was here, she'd vote in favour of it,' said Julia Soames, hoping to sway the balance by her friend's credentials.

Jennifer Sykes had taken the Sixth Form to see a film she had assured Graystone was *not* about Gay Christians in Paris.

'But you can't vote for someone who isn't here; it's not democratic,' retaliated Richard Smith. 'Besides, Peter isn't here, and I know the Art department would rather spend the money on clay. So that's one vote against, as well.'

'I didn't know supply teachers had a vote,' said Katy, supporting Dick.

'In that case,' Graystone triumphed, 'the opposition lose three more votes!'

'Actually, they can,' said Grace.

'Ah . . . then with the absentee voters, that's twenty-eight votes for each side. Hm . . .' Graystone scratched the mole on the side of his neck; it always itched when he was under stress.

'The deciding vote should go to Ken,' added a helpful Hewitt.

Graystone agreed. 'Well, as you know, Ken is away at another meeting, but he's designated his casting vote on all matters of importance to me. The result therefore stands at twenty-nine votes to twenty-eight, in favour of buying a staff photocopier. Material in specific conjunction with official school business will be free of charge; 3.5p per sheet will be the charge made for unofficial business. Paper may be purchased from Edwards & Son, 34 Allinson Place. Any questions?'

There were none. Graystone's eloquent delivery was evidence that he had thoroughly researched his project. It was indeed a kind, thoughtful gesture on his part; who could fail to be impressed? Following a long, preening pause, Graystone knew he had to continue. There was a more delicate matter. His voice dropped in pitch in an effort to render the question as relatively meaningless. Capriciously he asked, 'Who will take charge?

'You know, I mean . . . someone will have to be there when things go wrong . . . keep an eye out for strange happenings, check paper supplies . . . call for the engineer and so on.'

If anyone had felt himself a suitable applicant for the post prior to this speech, his spirits would sink on hearing of the dreary tasks the appointment involved. Graystone was silent. Not daring to speak, he fixed his anxious eyes on a dilating inkspot that had dripped from his pen. It was more than he could hope for. Silence. The whispering of his name . . . if only they would utter it a little louder. He willed them further.
Geoff Symms finally spoke out. 'Well . . . uh . . . I suppose you'd be the best person for it, Harold . . . knowing so much about it already.'

Graystone smiled and shrugged his shoulders, embarrassed. 'Hm . . . well, you know, I mean . . .'

It was decided. Large, proud in stature and filled with a sense of destiny, Graystone packed his briefcase and declared the meeting closed.

Law and Order in the Stable

PUNISH: to cause (one) to suffer for an offence: to cause one to suffer for (offence): to handle, beat, severely.
PUNISHMENT: act or method of punishing: penalty imposed for an offence: severe handling.

Horses are seldom vicious by nature alone, and what can be termed 'bad habits' are frequently acquired early on, which makes them difficult to break.

The golden rule is always SAS: be Sensible And Sympathetic. But above all, be firm. First find the cause of the trouble and then proceed to tackle the problem. If it is dealt with in the preliminary stages, you will probably have no cause to resort to drastic methods of correction at a later date.

Sometimes, horses start bad habits through sheer boredom; others are simply idle; and some pick them up in imitation of their fellow

50

creatures. Regular work must be given to horses and a net of hay provided for them to pick at during less active moments. Allow them no opportunity of passing bad habits on to others.

Whipping-Boy

> *One for sorrow*
> *Two for joy*
> *Three for a girl*
> *And four for a boy*

It was not what others might be saying that had bothered the young Kenneth Salmon; not even what his father might say or do when the information was conveyed. It was his own personal humiliation that he could not bear: the physical shame that marked his body; a body that, until then, he had felt to be in harmony with another part of himself: maybe his spirit. The beating he received in school had split them apart. Recently, he had written a heading in an exercise book – 'How the atom is split' – and although he did not altogether understand the logistics of the operation, he now experienced what felt like that same splitting process within himself. He felt shamed because his physical self had let his other half down. His face was red; his eyes burned; his hands stung; and with the consciousness of each new pain as the stick cracked, he saw more distinctly the back of a figure in his mind, walking away from wherever it had been. If only the beating would stop, so that he could follow the figure, catch it and bring it back before it separated itself forever. But it moved quickly, and he knew that in the sudden silence when the final lash had clipped the air, the figure would have disappeared. Suddenly it was over. He strained his eyes and watched the small black dot shrinking in the distance; but he knew by then that he was too late.

It seemed he never felt clean after that. He began to ask his mother for a clean shirt every morning and insisted on having his tie washed once a week. He polished his badges and cleaned his shoes more regularly. Still the shame did not leave him. 'It wasn't my fault, I didn't do it,' he repeated to himself, pleading

51

with it to go away; but it had no regard for truth. He bore the scar, that was all that mattered.

Salmon sat in his office and recalled with the same feeling of shame, the expression on his parent's faces when he told them of the punishment. 'It wasn't my fault, I didn't do it,' he repeated, though not for them. But for his father, the scar was sufficient evidence of guilt. 'Lazy', 'inconsiderate', 'lacked true competitive spirit', 'preferred kicking to learning' . . . He would wash his hands of him. And did.

Now Salmon tried again, as it seemed he had been doing all his life, to pull the two strings of his physical and invisible self together. He wanted to draw them tight so that they might contain him like the contents of a purse. He would be safe in a purse. But even as he tried, he felt the gap between the two widening: something stronger than both, forcing them apart.

He remembered on the night of the fatal punishment how he had hidden under his bedclothes, imagining himself to be in a purse. God's purse. It was the obvious choice of object, considering how many Days in the Life of pounds, shillings and pence he had been forced to write about since he started school. But now the purse-strings would not pull together. He caught hold of them on either side of him, but always this third thing was in the way: a new limb reaching out towards the light: another part of him turning nomad and moving off in a different direction.

CHAPTER FOUR

EXERCISE, WORK AND SUSTENANCE

A horse in good condition requires at least two hours of exercise daily, and for a working animal, adequate rest is essential. When resting, there should be quiet in the stable and no one should be allowed near the boxes. This ensures that horses are kept at the top of their condition. The greater part of the exercise should be carried out at walking pace, trotting only for about a quarter of the time. A horse in soft condition must not be worked hard, whether under saddle or in harness; it must be brought into work gradually. A major source of accidents and illness in the stable is often the result of the working of a tired or unfit animal.

Certain conditions must be observed if a fit, properly fed horse, is not to be overworked. The consideration shown by each rider to his/ her animal cannot be over-emphasised. The weight on the horse's back must not be too heavy and the riding pace not too fast. It must be remembered that the forelegs suffer greater concussion when travelling downhill, and on long rides, it is necessary to halt for a quarter of an hour every two or three hours. The horse should then be unsaddled and circulation restored to its back by massage or hand-slapping.

'Red House is better than Green.'

'Get stuffed, it ain't.'

'Blue's the best. They always win the Sports.'

'Get lost! Yellow wins the Sports.'

'Yellow! Yellow's the worst house of all.'

1C had taken advantage of what was officially termed a 'reading lesson' and continued to quarrel over the brightly coloured house badges they had received from their teachers that morning. Jonathan Hayward, who had introduced reading lessons to give his staff the opportunity to catch up on marking, once more resigned himself to the fact that Form One were growing up. House badges symbolized the first step towards the dissolution of first year innocence and harmony, creating a sense of permanency which inevitably brought about divided loyalties and therefore disruption. In primary school, competition had taken a temporary form: quiz teams arbitrarily selected by the teachers; regular changes of coloured ribbons to vary the strength of sports teams; rarely was a permanent mark made. But now, children bore a stamp which would remain with them until they left Riverside – Red, Yellow, Blue, Green – and these smaller divisions within the basic units of classes and sets fragmented the construction to an irreversible degree.

It was not until the weeks leading up to Christmas, when the complete lack of a central body to organize festivities became apparent, that houses, head boy and girl, prefects and other affiliated bodies, were deemed necessary. There were dances and parties to organize; the internal Christmas post; decoration of classrooms; most important, the readers for the Carol Service. Malcolm Hewitt again wondered why P.E. teachers were never chosen. He added up the number of staff, as he did every year, with that of pupils, and divided the number by nine, the maximum number of lessons that would be read on the big day. The odds on his being given one were again minuscule.

Among staff, house divisions were deeply entrenched. Many had been affiliated to the same house for over ten years, having refused to surrender the colours to which they had belonged in the old grammar school. Graystone continued to wear a blue badge every day, despite the unwritten school rule that senior staff should not involve themselves with house politics. Solidarity was shown by defending one's own children, even if they were in the wrong; hence the punishment administered to a Green would be a light one, if given by a Green member of staff. In this way, the Reds, Yellows, Blues and Greens among the staff acted as mini-unions to support the claims of the members of the main organization. There was always considerable anticipation in the SCR as teachers awaited the house lists and the names of house leaders.

54

'I have taken it upon myself to devise a temporary list during the Headmaster's . . . uh . . . incapacitation,' said Graystone, pinning a neatly typed notice on the board.

Staff gathered round.

'Well, Dick's creeping finally paid off.'

'Young! He'll never be sober enough to hold a house assembly.'

'Hmph! As usual, only one token woman.'

Newcomers to the important leadership posts were greeted with either approval or antipathy, according to who had been demoted from the previous year. Only Jonathan Hayward had held on to his old position as head of Green House.

'I'm in your house, Sir,' called Jane Ellis from the back of his class, renewing the debate.

'And me, Sir!'

'And me!'

'Greens are the best, aren't they, sir?'

'Get on with your work – NOW! And quietly,' said Hayward.

The class again settled.

Hayward looked around the class while his pupils continued to work. He noticed the deepening shadows under several pairs of tired eyes and tried to recall his own first term at secondary school. He could remember the routines themselves, but not any feeling he experienced in relation to them. As a teacher, he found it hard to believe that all pupils did not hate the routine of school life. The days seemed longer, yet he still pitied the children who, to him, looked physically incapable of sustaining themselves over the long distance. But they did not question it any more than he had when he was their age; it was all taken for granted: you went to school; likes and dislikes played no part in the routine. The rebels were simply the few who could not cope with it, and their retaliation not one against the establishment, but against their own inability to conform.

Hayward supposed that the compliance of the majority was like a state of prolonged grief: you coped because your body suddenly found the resources to handle that which, in normal circumstances, appeared difficult to face. Imagine if, at the age of four, someone outlined the educational process to the prospective pupil: well, you go to a building for . . . ooh, anything from twelve to fourteen years, most days of the year between the hours of nine and four. It would sound like having to do time; a punishment for being born. He longed for that childhood sense of timelessness again and envied these pupils their unconscious reliance on those inner resources. This whole process of growth of knowledge would change all that: not the passion of knowledge itself, but the attempts at comprehension of it which would be forced upon them as they grew older. And the more their field of knowledge widened, the greater their questioning and increased lack of comprehension would be. Now, in the lack of knowledge, their innocence, they were in control within the boundaries of their world, where experience took the form of an intuitive understanding rather than a set of factual data. Growth of knowledge extended those boundaries; feelings could no longer be contained or controlled. Real experience was the degree of intensity with which you explored – and held on to – your feelings. Suddenly Hayward felt that he wanted to teach nothing to any class – even that he had nothing to teach them. He resented the system in its assumption that childhood innocence was synonymous with ignorance, a lack of organized knowledge. At the same time, he was frightened: you have the facts, the eyes in front of him seemed to say, but you're nothing more than a child dressing up, playing a game. They were humouring him just like real grown-ups.

Basic Exercises

FORM: 1T   PHYSICS   CHRISTMAS EXAMINATIONS 1983

TIME: 1 HOUR

Read through all the questions carefully before answering.

Answer all questions

1. a)   Write out the following passage and fill in your answers

56

where there are spaces. Please underline them.

Thomas Edison was born in the year . . . . at Milan in . . . . Although he was deaf from the age of . . . ., he was able to hear the . . . . and later learnt . . . . His first job as an operator was in a bookshop at . . . . and after various developments in this area he then became a full-time . . . .

b) Name two of Edison's inventions. Explain their uses and, where possible, use diagrams to illustrate your answer.

c) Give three reasons why the second half of Edison's life was less successful than the first.

2. a) What is the dictionary definition of an electric charge?
   b) Draw a basic electrical circuit.
   c) How is it possible to collect electricity from the air and what might it be used for?

3. You are a young inventor. Describe your latest invention that shows the power of electricity being used in a harmful or dangerous way (higher marks will be given for imaginative inventions).

NAME: Andrew Wells

1) Thomas Edison was born in the year *1847* at Milan in *Ohio*. Although he was deaf from the age of *12*, he was able to hear the *telegraph* and later learnt *telegraphy*. His first job as an operator was in a bookshop at *Port Huron* and after various developments in this area he then became a full-time inventor.

NAME: Alan Colby

1b)   The electric rat trapper caught rats.

Lights gave light.

1c)   His second life was not so sucesfull as the first one
because he spent a lot of money and his factries were
burnt and he ran out of things to invent.

NAME: Simon Laing

2a)   The dictionry defanition of an electric change is something that is changed with electricity.

2b)   BROWN . . . . BLUE

2c)   Electric can be cauht in the air in big ~~brushes~~ combs but
it is no good and can't be used for nothing.

NAME: Timothy Leach

3) My latest invention is a sort of electric brush. It is made of
nylon and if you put it against a cat's fur it will brush very
fast. Sparks will jump from the fur to the brush. The brush
will go faster and there will be more and more sparks until
the cat catches fire. It is called the Catrifier.

Biting and Kicking

Boredom and a lack of work is often a cause of kicking. Mares are more prone to the vice than geldings, and particular care must be taken and allowances made during the mare's oestrus period. Do not aggravate ticklish spots and do not use bullying tactics.

Biting is uncommon, although many horses like to make playful nips and snatches on occasion. Should this show signs of developing, however, it must not be aggravated by teasing. Again, be gentle on ticklish spots.

Many stallions are natural biters, and a particularly vicious one will lay back its ears, reveal the whites of its eyes and behave in an aggressive manner. Firm treatment will have little effect. Tie him up or use a muzzle or side-stick to restrict his movement.

Exercise Session

'Sir! Sir! Have you marked our papers yet?'

'No.'

'Aw, Sir.'

'Did I pass, Sir?'

'I just told you, I haven't marked them yet. Now sit down and be quiet.'

'When will you be marking them, Sir?'

'Belt up or I'll keep you in after school.'

'You've got to give twenty-four hours' notice for detention, Sir.'

Geoff Symms sat at his desk and waited for 3F to settle down. He hated Thursdays. It was the only day of the week when he didn't have a free lesson either before or after the lunch hour, so he was never able to down more than the minimum requirement of two pints he needed to get him through the school day. Even his form had to go without registration two afternoons a week.

'Sir, why are you eating Polos?'

'Have you been drinking, Sir?'

'Randall! If you don't shut up, I'll send you to see the Head.'

'Sorry, Sir!' The boy shouted his apology and looked around the room for approval.

'I'm not deaf.'

'*SIR!*' Randall shouted again.

Symms looked up. 'Take out your exercise books and turn to Friday's homework. Randall, come here.'

The boy swaggered from the back of the room. He met the teacher's eyes with defiance. 'Sir?' Now he was grinning.

'When I speak to you, you answer properly, is that clear?'

'I did, Sir.'

'Don't argue, Randall.'

'I'm not, Sir.'

'Shut *UP!*' said Symms, gripping the boy's right shoulder. 'Now just sit down and shut it.'

Randall smirked and returned to his seat. Symms faced the rest of the class. 'Hands up those who haven't done their homework.'

A dozen hands crawled up to half-mast, each representing a familiar excuse.

Sir, I didn't know it had to be in by today.

Sir, I've only done it in rough.

Sir, I've forgotten my book.

Sir, I lent my book to Steven and he's away.

Sir, I didn't get it.

'Come on, quickly. There's no need to make such a noise about it.'

Symms walked around, examining pupils' books. Nobody expected much from 3F; that's why, as Head of Geography, it was perfectly acceptable for him to be taking them for Biology. The scheme, which came under the title General Curriculum, had been devised by Graystone, the theory being that to increase harmony among teachers, they should be exposed to the difficulties involved with each other's subjects. 3F was thought to be good stamping-ground on which to try out the scheme: these were the pupils who couldn't tell the difference between subjects, they were hardly likely to notice a discrepancy in the teachers who taught them.

Symms read a little of Friday's homework from each book.

There are over six hundred species of spiders in this country. Their bodies are divided into two parts. They have eight legs and eight eyes. The spider preys on other creatures.

Andrew Simpson's incomprehensible handwriting. Unrecognizable blotches on Philip Buckman's book. Simon Thomas' enormous drawings on porridge-coated pages. Then Jackson.

The silk strands of a web are stronger than iron even though they're thin of one bit of a millimetre and if one piece spreads around the wood . . .

'What on earth's all that about? And it's world, not wood. Is it too much to ask you to copy a few sentences from a book? You're in Form Three, not the infants. Do it again, Jackson.'
'Aw, Sir.'
'*Again!*

. . . if spun right around the world, would weigh less than six ounces. When a spider uses a dry thread to approach its prey, it uses a sticky one to catch it.

Matthew Lucas, the boy sitting next to Tony Randall. Then large, bold letters and bright, wax crayon illustrations.

Spiders inject poison into their victims with their fangs. Afterwards, some wrap their prey in silk and carry them to their nests.

Tony Randall.

'That's a bit untidy, isn't it?'
'Didn't have time, Sir.'
'What's that supposed to mean?'
'Just didn't, Sir.' Randall looked around the class for encouragement. He found none.
'And what's this?'
'Fangs.'
'Fangs?'
'Spider's fangs.'
'The spider is an animal, not a vampire. You'll do it again, please. Neatly, this time.'
'Aw, no way, Sir.'
Symms clenched his fists. 'You'll do it again, or I'll . . . I'll . . .'

61

The boy stared at the teacher, his sharp, fang-like teeth defiant. 'What, Sir?' Saliva frothed on his lips. His eyes shone.

Symms lifted him out of his seat by grasping the back of his jumper and thrust him down the aisle to the front of the classroom.

'Now tell the whole class why *you* especially should be excused; why *you* in particular did not have the time to do your work properly; why *you*, Mr Tony Randall, are so special.'

' 'Cos I'm brainier,' said the boy, enjoying being the centre of attention.

Symms gripped Randall's shoulders again. 'One more word from you and you'll be . . . you'll be . . .'

Randall queried the threat with raised eyebrows; the whites of his eyes glared, beckoning anything the teacher had to offer. Symms tightened the grip on his victim's shoulder and in one sharp, angry movement, pushed him back against the blackboard. In the seconds that followed the smack of Randall's body against the black, the stillness was broken only by a mare's-tail of chalk dust, which rose in one quick and powerful burst before falling through the quiet.

Horsepower

> *Horsepower is the unit chosen for expressing the rate at which an engine gives out work or energy. The amount of work done can be measured by the distance through which a weight is lifted. EXAMPLE: if a boy weighing 7 stone (98 lbs) runs upstairs to a height of 15 feet, he does 98 × 15 or 1,470 foot-pounds of work. If it takes him six seconds to do this, then he has worked at the rate of 1,470 foot-pounds in 6 seconds. 6 seconds is contained 10 times in one minute, and therefore his rate of work will be 1,470 × 10, or 14,700 foot-pounds per minute. This is a little less than half horsepower. A boy, of course, could only keep up this pace for a few seconds. That is the important point to remember: a boy is only half as powerful as a horse.*

Extra-Curricular

Geoff Symms wished there was a way that teachers, like animal owners, could have their charges put down. What was everyone making such a fuss about? Hadn't he just hit a boy who got *on* his nerves, off? You couldn't win in this job. If pupils were undisciplined you got the blame, and if you tried to discipline them you also got the blame. They were lazy little bastards, all of them; they didn't know the meaning of hard work. No one in 3F would be sweating their way through university, and at the end of the day they'd be financially better off for it. So Randall had 'social problems' as they were now calling it. He wasn't an aggressive little sod any more but a 'deviant'.

The only perks in teaching were the girls. It was still a delight to witness how the unlikeliest pupils developed such enormous chests: little bespectacled and spotty creatures measuring 26″ in Form One somehow managed, by the time they reached the Lower Sixth, to grow the most remarkable feats of science. During the summer months, when the Sixth Form block in particular became unbearably warm, Symms refused to open windows in the hope that girls might be forced to remove their blazers. Then the sweat would continent across the white, flimsy school shirts, revealing the horizon of a breast underneath. Oh, how he looked forward to those summers. And how he regretted the failure of his campaign to have the long summer holiday period moved to February.

They were also so willing, these inexperienced nymphets. They were always offering to help you tidy your stockroom and, being a Geography cupboard in Symms' case, it was always so easy to throw a few maps around and untidy it should a young lady request some overtime. It was easy to pick these girls up after school, too. They shyly accepted lifts home and didn't mind if you took the long route or found yourself lost down a deserted farm-track. Fortunately, Symms had an understanding wife who didn't mind the extent to which he became involved in extra-curricular activities. Drama, the Poetry Society, Debating, Creative Writing, Choir, Orchestra – he devoted all his time and energy to school life and was rewarded with a steady supply of young mistresses. He took a full week to explain to each of them everything he knew about sex, and he rejoiced in the knowledge that so many had been able to share the breadth of his learning.

He knew that less attractive colleagues, probably with a mixture of jealousy and secret admiration, called him a pervert. Symms preferred to think of himself as a fertilizer: spreading himself over much ground, each term bringing new crop to fruition. A fervert, if you like.

This term, he had been working on Sandra Carson of Form Five. Giving her low marks for essays in the hope that she would ask for extra tuition failed, when she announced that her father taught Geography in a university and was greatly distressed at the tough standards being set his daughter. She didn't have a very good grasp of the meaning of 'tidying' the stockroom, either. Having asked for her assistance after school one afternoon, Symms arrived ten minutes after the final bell had rung, only to find every shelf perfectly stacked and the girl gone. This time he planned to be there when she arrived, and it was there he waited, tearing pages from a set of *Geography Can Be Fun* and slipping them untidily between the pages of copies of *Equatorial Landscapes*. He also emptied a box labelled *Maps of the World* onto the floor: this guaranteed her having to bend down at some point, a position from which it would be far easier to manoeuvre her onto her back.

The only problem with the whole event, which had been meticulously planned, was that it was Sandra Carson's first contact with the male anatomy. Scooping the maps into a tidy pile on the floor, she was unsure how to react when Symms, kneeling beside her, caught hold of her hand and pressed it to his groin. Sandra was familiar with the dried prune resting between her brother's legs because she had seen it during the bathtimes they shared together as children, but as far as she remembered, the area where her hand was now resting bore no resemblance to it. Symms undid his trousers and slid her hand inside his underpants. God, this was *nothing* like her brother's. What was she supposed to do with it? It didn't feel like an object of great aesthetic beauty, and the changing of its shape and texture made it increasingly difficult, given her position, to keep hold with any degree of comfort. Suddenly she wanted to go home. She had Maths, French and English homework to do, and now she had missed the school bus. Symms, sensing a lull in the proceedings, hastened the action forward, placing his own hand on the girl's and motioning it back and forth. He knew he was a good teacher. He felt like a parent teaching his child to play 'Go and Tell Aunt Nancy' on the recorder. Eventually, after touching all the wrong notes, the fingers went in the right places and there was the promise of greater tunes to come. Miss Carson remained somewhat baffled. She wondered at the urgency with which the teacher grabbed a map of the world and the exact nature of the lava that flowed from his body, flooding the whole of Southern America. The teacher explained, in summarized form, the working process of penial irrigation, and for this time at least, Aunt Nancy would never get to hear that the old grey goose was dead.

'Right . . . Jesus, try to sound a bit more enthusiastic about it all. These are your Chosen People; they're very hungry and it's *your fault*. They've come to listen to *you*, and for some obscure reason you've chosen a hill stuck in the middle of nowhere with not a Sainsbury's in sight. Sound as if you *care*, for goodness' sake. They're *hungry*.'

'Miss – don't you think the hunger's symbolic?'

'Judas! Stop looking for symbols and find some damned food.'

The disciples started to weave among The Crowd who were assembled at Jesus' feet.

'Look interested!' shouted Liz Caversham to a boy picking his nose.

' "Here is a boy with five barley loaves and . . ." '

'Miss – he's away.'

'Why didn't you tell me before? Right – you – yes, you with the uh . . .' (She could hardly say 'the acne') '. . . . the brown hair.'

'Me, miss?'

'No! You. Right. Start again.'

' "Here is a boy with five barley loaves and . . ." ' The boy handed an object to the disciple – 'a Mars bar!'

The Crowd erupted into hysterical laughter. Liz Caversham was losing patience.

'Simon Peter – I am tired of your silly behaviour at every single rehearsal. Now shut up or I'll make you a leper.'

'But miss, he . . .'

'Do not quarrel amongst yourselves,' said Jesus, raising his hand.

'Shut up, Jesus! Now grow up, both of you – and sons of God

do *not* bite their nails! We'll take it from the top again –
"Master, master, the crowd is hungry . . ." '

The Drama department had three weeks left to rehearse its
Christmas production, *Godspell*. The cast, selected mainly from
the Upper School, was at the stage of rehearsal when the
novelty and initial excitement has worn off, and anticipation of
performance is still far ahead. Nothing gelled. Mary Magda-
lene had grown shy of kissing Jesus' hand; Judas was paranoid
and had failed his Latin test; and Jesus had fallen in love with
his mother.

' "Here is a boy with five barley sugars . . ." '

'Peter!'

'It was an accident, honest, miss. I'll do it again . . . "Here is
a *boy* . . . *Here* is a boy . . ." ' Simon Peter was doubled over with
laughter.

'Quickly, Peter is starving to death,' whispered Jesus.

'I've lost a contact lens,' said Mary Magdalen.

'I feel sick,' said the boy with five barley loaves and two small
fishes.

'Right! We'll leave it there for today.' Liz Caversham knew
from experience that they would get no further. But The Line
had been found: the one line that bonds a cast together in their
anticipation of the actor's attempt to deliver it without
laughter. They had advanced. The sheep, albeit a black one,
had been found. The cast was now a company.

Geoff Symms, who was helping out in the props' department,
waited beside his car while pupils left the rehearsal hall. The
Virgin Mary, who alas had opted for Physics, Maths and
Chemistry 'A' Levels, saw him on her way to the toilet.

'Can I give you a lift?' he called.

She walked in the direction of the car. 'Do you go in my
direction?'

'I can do. Come here a minute.' Symms beckoned to the girl
to join him under the oak tree beside the Science Laboratory.
'You were very good tonight,' he said, pulling her to him. 'The
part of Mary requires that special something: a certain
vulnerability, an innocence, desire held in check by reverence.
You've got that something.'

'Have I?'

'Mmm,' Symms lowered his face to meet the girl's. He closed his eyes and opened his mouth to consume once more the familiar taste of young blood. But just as his lips reached hers, Mary drew back her right leg and with all the force that is gainly in the mother of Christ, rammed her knee into Symms' groin.

'Sorry, no room at the inn,' she explained and, joined by John the Baptist carrying her satchel, she left Symms to his cries under the oak.

Health and Nutrition

If horses are to perform at their best, it is vital that adequate provision be made for their nourishment. Diet is often an important factor in determining the behaviour of a horse, and for this reason, utmost care must be taken over nutrition.

It is as well to adopt a special system of feeding from as early on as possible and look out for changes in behaviour that might be attributable to diet. When deciding upon a system of feeding, there are several circumstances that must be taken into account: age, constitution, temperament, work, the time of year, weather conditions etc. Knowledge and experience must be backed up by intelligent observation of each animal.

Miss Marchmont was chosen from a shortlist of three other candidates. She was the only one who was given four 5.9s and two straight sixes on the governors' mark-sheets for General Impression. In the individual categories – breath, finger-nails, complexion, teeth, and pupils of eyes, she was awarded a further ten straight sixes. It was decided. Miss Marchmont was the obvious choice. She was offered the post of Chief Cook that very afternoon, and accepted.

Not that she had ever been in doubt regarding the suitability of her own credentials. She knew she had excellent references, was of immaculate appearance, and possessed the ability to set up an instant rapport between herself and an interviewer, giving herself as she would to a good, full-blooded piece of topside. She also knew that they would be impressed by her attending the interview in her cook's dress and matching apron and cap, freshly laundered and stiffly starched. It showed that she was totally committed to her work, so much so that she felt a change of clothing would exhibit extravagance on her part. The other candidates revealed no such qualities: a young slip of a girl with a red nose (imagine how *that* would look in a steamy kitchen, thought Miss Marchmont); a fat, elderly woman (obesity was always a bad sign – they would never know where she might be dipping her fingers); and a woman with a stammer *and* a lisp (which would never do – she could be hours just giving out instructions to s-sauté the s-sausages in the s-saucepan, not to mention the saliva that would be going in with them). They had made the right decision, she was certain. What was it the Chairman had said when he offered her the post . . . ? She had a certain 'Je ne sais croissant'.

Miss Marchmont joined Riverside in September, 1971, and from the start she was given the nickname 'Matron'. It was as if the dull, lifeless ingredients came in at the *Outpatients* side door, and after the healing hand of Matron had been laid upon them, they were born again. By the time they were discharged to the canteen in their new form, they had again reached peak condition.

Matron's first job was to rid the grammar school kitchen of the Old in order to bring in the New. She threw away all utensils and pans that showed the smallest signs of ageing, and discovered, much to her disgust, pieces of food that had dried and stuck in small crevices at the bottom of tureens. She tested every fork against a glass bowl and if the prongs did not ring out with a perfect 'G', the cutlery too was discarded. The store-cupboard was completely cleared, and items marked 'Use before January 1965' burned on the caretaker's weekly bonfire. Sub-committees were appointed amongst the kitchen staff, and a list of separate tasks under the general heading 'Surgery' was set for each group: clear out dead mice, cement mouse holes, destroy all products that contained artificial preservatives and colouring, pull down cobwebs and reaccommodate homeless spiders in classrooms . . . it seemed there was no end to the extent of the operation she was having to perform. But after three long, arduous weeks, Matron was in absolute control of her ward.

Her routine began at 6.30 a.m., in her bathroom, where she scooped out the half-moons of dirt from beneath her finger-nails, scrubbed each nail until it glowed with pinky-white, pearl-like softness, and finally, with the same hard brush, brought up the ribs of flesh around the joints to stiff red folds. She knew that every day her hands held the potential to cause either great joy or great sadness and it was essential, therefore, to keep them in perfect condition. What if, for instance, through neglect on her part, an excess of dirt in one finger-nail became mixed in with the grease she rubbed on a pastry tin? A child might eat the pastry in all innocence and wonder then at his feeling of nausea, just as he was being questioned on the Battle of Trafalgar. He might stumble over his words, the teacher interpret this as neglect of homework; accuse him, demand an explanation. The child, on feeling the sickness rise, would remain silent; the teacher grow more angry, send the boy to the Head for punishment. The Head might decide to cane him – once, for neglect of homework, twice for insolence. Then the parents might complain – and justly so; take the case to the European Rights Commission, keep the child away from school for the duration of the case, resulting in loss of work, failed 'O' Levels . . . Matron knew there was no end to what might ensue as a result of dirty grease on a pastry tin. To make provision for such accidents, she set up, in the kitchen annexe, a counselling service for staff and pupils, where kitchen-related problems could be rectified before they got out of hand. It included a service by which spots could be professionally squeezed, the extract analysed and a special diet be constructed for the individual concerned.

Matron arrived at the school promptly at 8 a.m. in order to inspect the kitchen for cleanliness and general appearance, despite having checked it three times at the end of the previous day. She loved that morning smell of emptiness, the shine of smooth, clean surfaces, the early song of hungry cutlery. When her staff arrived, she watched with pleasure – an artist before a blank canvas – the colours and shapes mount the bare surfaces like oils, under the brushes, spoons and spatulas of her staff. Before the cooks began work, Matron strictly supervised the scrubbing of their nails and hands, again performing like a surgeon on her own. Then she lined them up in order of height to inspect the whiteness of their overalls and the tidiness of their hair.

There were more pupils and staff wanting school dinners at Riverside than ever there had been during the days of the grammar school. It was the envy of neighbouring schools for the way it was able to keep pupils in during the lunch-hours; they just didn't want to leave the premises. Once they had finished their meals, many continued to loiter around low, open windows, or climb drainpipes to higher ones, trying until the last possible moment to inhale Matron's appetising odours. One boy had even fallen when he leaned a little too far in an attempt to sniff the steam coming out of the ventilators on the roof. His spine was broken in three places, Matron boasted to her sister.

At least half an hour before the bell went for lunch at 12.30 p.m., a queue of Sixth Form pupils and staff fortunate enough to have a free lesson at the end of the morning, would form outside the hatch in the canteen. Some pupils mitched off lessons or affected sickness in order to establish an early place in the queue, and staff with a free lesson waited anxiously before the notice-board in the morning, hoping that their 'free' would not be taken for supervision. If it was they tried to swop with someone else, but such exchanges were rare. If a transaction *did* take place, the other member of staff usually asked for a bonus, maintaining that the surrender of a pre-lunch lesson was too great a sacrifice and should therefore go with the taking of an afternoon break supervision in addition to another lesson. Sometimes the bonus took a more devious form: staff were asked to lie as to the whereabouts of their colleagues, should they not appear to be on school premises during their 'frees'. 'He was here a minute ago' and 'I've only just seen her' were among the most popular phrases used. Only once was a flagrant lie detected, when Mr Holloway, a French teacher, was killed in a car-crash three miles away at 11.40 a.m. during fourth lesson, his 'free'.

If there was one word that could be chosen to describe the attraction of Matron's food, it would be *physical*. So physical, in fact, that often the staff forgot to remember the taste. It was always the visual image that struck them so forcibly. The head of art said that it gave him the feeling he had when gazing upon a painting by Goya – of being invited in, and then, unable to draw himself away. Even the food that had always been a traditional part of the school menu took on new physical perspective: sugary, even-cupped breasts of full sponge-like doughnuts with sticky, jam-red nipples: small, saucer shaped Yorkshire puddings, the batter evenly distributed, sturdy as Dutch caps; the warm, fleshy wombs of moist baked apples, sultanas like tiny embryos threading their way down the core, the main uterine passage; mushrooms, smooth and pointed as the tips of circumcised penises; chicken succulent as a slice of baby's roasted buttock; chocolate pudding ducking on spoons like a strong black body pulling on its mate; the soft tongues of cling peaches, slippery as goldfish; butterfly cakes with perfectly split, vulva-like wings, butter icing foaming at the join; white sauce creamy as semen and only half the calories. Yes, physical was the very word.

Every day, the menu included a main meal – a dinner and sweet – in addition to the full range of individual items on sale in the canteen. The food of the meal symbolised a different member of staff each day, and after lunch, teachers were invited to pay 5p to guess who had been represented. The results were announced at a quarter to four and a free meal ticket issued to the lucky winners who had guessed correctly.

Sometimes Matron chose to represent the strengths (such as alphabet spaghetti in pots that made up eight-syllabled words, to symbolise the literacy of Miss White of the English department, who could do *The Times* crossword) and at other times the weaknesses (discoloured liver, a symbol of Mr Young's rumoured alcoholism) of her chosen character. Or, if she was in a devious mood, she chose an event that could be associated with a particular person. When she discovered a previous Woodwork teacher was to have his leg amputated, she made one-legged ginger-bread men; and when Mr Holloway had his accident, she left the dead, staring eyes in the pieces of fish, crushed the bones inside, and made a blood-red cocktail sauce to pour over the top. No one guessed correctly. Richard Smith demanded his money back and said that it wasn't fair, that dead people didn't count. Matron grudgingly gave it back. What a spoilsport he was. Some people just had no sense of fun.

End of the Season

Lost Property

2 duffle coats
3 pairs of gym shoes
1 pair of trainers
1 orthodontic brace
1 shirt
1½ English textbooks
1 pornographic magazine (soft)
2 cider bottles (empty)
1 packet of cigarettes
1 glass eye (brown)

Kenneth Salmon wanted to go to sleep for the rest of the winter. When he lay down, his body instinctively curled into hibernation; he felt the pull of muscles at the back of his neck as his head folded onto his chest; his hands clawed to his body in the position of pre-birth. It took nothing more than the thought of human contact for the shape to form. He felt for changes in the muscles of his face, the texture of his skin, but there was only the shrinking feeling inside to tell him that it was the middle of winter. Each time he went out, he felt stripped of his skin, believing that the merest glance could injure him as if he were an open wound. He flinched at the touch of everyday life which carried on around him, regardless. It was all too busy and too loud. Yes. He would sleep out the rest of the winter.

Winter surrounds him like a mask. He is the wind; he is the bare trees; he is a black footprint in the snow. No one can see him, hidden in winter. In sleep, he is camouflaged and he rests unnoticed at the foot of a tree.

This is the best trick of all, children. Your headmaster can make himself disappear. At the flick of a switch, a light goes out. Your headmaster is a miracle of science.

He hears an orchestra downstairs: at first, single notes – a string that may be in the living-room; a scale on a clarinet; and a thump thump thump he has never heard before. He hears them as he might an early morning radio in another room. His pillow is hot. He turns it, and within a minute the orchestra is silenced in a cool cheek. The dribble of sleep runs down his chin.

He watches his dream. He counts to ten and the figure he is watching runs away to hide. He stalks its shadow in a building that is a school, or a hospital, void of all other life. He comes face to face. Himself. But runs away before . . .

He opens his eyes and tries to remember what day it is. Yesterday held nothing to distinguish it from any other, and today he cannot remember what he has to do. There is no indication in the white alarm clock on the bedside table, nor in the grey of sky in the 'v' between the curtains. The curve of his wife's back beside him is any day, every day; her slow breathing is yesterday, today and tomorrow. The white frill of her nightdress has fallen from one shoulder; her scalp is carelessly imprisoned by hair grips. But to which day does she belong? And how can he find out?

He feels too heavy for the morning. Lying awake, he listens to his breath in the rise and fall of his rib-cage. Every sound is too loud; every movement too large. His weight swells with every breath.

Yes. It is Sunday. He has taken to staying in bed on Sunday morning. His wife tells their daughter not to disturb him, and for the whole of the morning he listens to the sound of his body.

But it is not Sunday, after all. At a quarter to seven, the alarm rings. Every day he reaches out and accidentally knocks it over, though for twenty years it has been in the same place. He listens to the tick and composes it into the rhythm of a nursery rhyme: Ba – tick – ba – tick – black – tick – sheep – tick. His wife rolls onto her back and he looks for the day in her half open mouth. He thinks, for the first time in his life, that she is an ugly woman.

How will he find out what day this is, with no memory of

73

yesterday? His body will know; already it is trying to step out of bed; but how does the message reach his brain and bring him into consciousness? His brain has forgotten how to talk. He does not receive the signal that would enable him to help his body carry out its desire to get up. He must wait until a memory returns: the memory that yesterday his secretary told him that there was one more day to go, which he will link to the memory of Christmas. Suddenly he will know that today is Friday and that it is the last day of term.

He unpacked another box. It was all beginning to look terribly complicated. He would have to go back to tackling things the way he had been taught at school; the way he had taught his pupils. First he needed to make a list of his materials, stating at the side of each its purpose in the construction as a whole. He would need to check each part individually, so that when it came to the final working, he would not be let down by the smallest fault. Every year, at home, the lights for the Christmas tree failed to work, the effect of the whole having been let down by one fault. But he would make sure that this was all in perfect working order. He quickly tapped his finger against a live wire and took pleasure in its sting. He tested the length of another piece between the wall and his desk. From his position on the floor, he noticed a shadow blocking the light at the foot of his door. Slowly he crawled across, and at the last moment leapt to his feet and quickly pulled open the door.

Graystone jumped back from where he had been trying to peep through the keyhole. 'Ah, Ken . . . I . . . uh . . . just wanted a word. It's about the final assembly.'

'Yes?'

'Are you going to be taking the service?'

'Why not?'

'It's just that I . . . uh . . . Could we have a word?'

'Certainly.'

Graystone took a step forward, as if he had a right to access with a search warrant.

'Out here will be fine,' said Salmon, blocking his entry.

'I just wanted to know if you're feeling better.'

'Better?'

74

'Well, you know, I mean, you've been a bit under the weather. We haven't seen a lot of you.'

'Never felt better,' said Salmon. 'I just have a lot of work on. You know how it is at the end of term.' What an ugly man, he thought, mentally plucking Graystone's eyebrows.

'Well, if you're sure.'

'Absolutely.' And what big ears he had.

'You'll be doing the assembly, then?'

'Of course.'

Graystone sighed. He would have liked to have led a major event at Yuletide.

Salmon returned to his room and closed the door. Suddenly he stopped. Fear crossed his face. The string. It was twisted. Which way had he turned when he re-entered the room? Right. Therefore another turn to the left should unravel him . . . No, now he felt more tangled than ever. That meant he would need two turns to the right to unravel himself back to his original starting position . . .

For weeks he had not been able to escape the feeling that he was attached to a piece of string. It seemed to come from the centre of his body and was fixed permanently to a point up ahead. It had made life in school extremely difficult. It was not that he *would* not participate in activities as fully as he once had, but that he *could* not. There was always so much walking about, turning to speak to stray voices, journeying the complex meanderings of so many corridors and stairways. All were unconducive to his being able to cope with this new restriction. He had not chosen it; it had struck him like a sudden illness. Just one day, when buying a few groceries after school, he had felt, on turning to look into the freezer of vegetables, a strange pulling around his waist. He turned a little further and felt an adjustment to his bodily weight that was not righted until he stood up straight again and faced the direction in which he had been travelling. After that, he had been very careful with the supermarket trolley on future occasions. It was one thing to tangle himself up, but there was no need to involve other people. Only once had he got into real difficulty, when the coffee and tea had been transferred to different shelves. He always saved them until last to avoid the risk of tying up the pyramids of baked beans, but when they were not in their usual

75

place, he was forced to double back. Half an hour later, he was still at the yoghurts, where an old woman had asked him to read a label. He turned to speak, moved to look at the carton under a better light, and then caught sight of a new brand of chocolate biscuits . . . Soon he was hopelessly knotted. A few people passed him sympathetic nods and glances when they saw him rotating first one way, then the other, in his predicament. People were very understanding in that way.

There was spaghetti bolognese for the last lunch of the term; there were no winners for guessing the correct symbol. Matron smiled and prided herself both on her wit and her observation.

Godspell had been a huge success and Liz Caversham showed sufficient surprise when she was handed the bouquet she always received at final performances. The organization of the Christmas examinations had been as great a success for Roy Dixon, and only one class had ended up sitting the wrong paper. The mistake was discovered after an hour, when Anthony Grose of Form Two had an asthma attack from the shock of not being able to answer one question. At the Upper School dance, Geoff Symms was observed dancing a little too closely to Sandra Carson, and Malcolm Hewitt cracked two ribs in splitting up a fight. It more than made up for his not reading in the Carol Service. Matron provided a lavish banquet for the staff party which, apart from the vomit found in the car-park the following day ('Frozen solid,' the caretaker had said) and a dent in Andrew Young's new Volvo, had gone extremely well. Harold Graystone collapsed with a heart-attack; Timothy Leach stopped wetting himself; and Reverend Rook mislaid God. During the holidays, a parent of a girl in Form Three would choke to death on a turkey bone; two pupils would steal a Christmas tree and be fined; and Kenneth Salmon would wake early on Christmas morning in time to see Father Christmas making his journey back across the sky.

On 25 December, he will open his eyes and know that it is Christmas Day.

CHAPTER FIVE

THE SPRING SEASON

DARK HORSE: enigma, mystery, unknown quantity, skeleton in the cupboard, sealed book.

'Morning, H.G. Glad to be back?' greeted Geoff Symms.

'I'm not sure that "glad" is the word,' answered Graystone, wondering at the sudden familiarity of 'H.G.' He did not like Symms. How could anyone be a competent head of department at twenty-nine? It was ridiculous. Teaching was a profession you had to be broken into; Symms was a mere foal. Graystone liked the analogy and made a mental note to include it in his next county bulletin.

Other members of staff followed in a steady trickle of remonstrance: Grace Calne, Katy Ekkart and Dick Smith; and Hilary Williams, a wind musician, whose lunch-time practices were greatly unappreciated by her colleagues.

'But you know, as Aristotle says,' Graystone continued, ' "He who is unable to live in society . . . must either be a beast or a god." '

Symms nodded, forgetting what had elicited this response. But at the word 'god', Graystone's attention had already been diverted to the table heralding the new photocopier. He moved towards it, leaving behind the idle chatter of his colleagues. This was it. He laid his hand, trembling, on the red plastic forehead; ran his fingers over the dialled eyes and round to the gaping mouth. This was his toy. He was commander of its every gurgle. He thought back to the day of his election and smiled benignly at the cold face in the corner of the room, impassioned with a sense of his own importance and duty towards the machine. An ugly, monstrous addition, grumbled many who

77

saw it; but not Harold Graystone. His eyes feasted luxuriously on the smooth skin, the shining face. The term had just begun.

It was essential to read the instruction booklet if the machine was to be in good working order by break. Graystone perched himself within close proximity of the side panel, which he flicked open and shut like a wing, assessing any superhuman qualities the machine might possess. When he thought he had tapped the combination that would bring the alien to life, he went off to find Miss Beak, Resources, in her stock-room.

Miss Beak's job was the most important one in the school. She could see it in no other light. A crisp, white overall, smelling of efficiency, rustled its starch against her busy form as she marched from one end of the school to the other. She spoke with the tone of a Girl Guide leader and walked with her body tilted at an angle. When she turned corners, her body lurched so far on a sideways diagonal that it gave the impression she would fall over completely; but then, with the elasticity of a boxer's punch-bag, she returned to centre. On hearing the official squelch of her shoes outside the door, several staff automatically stood to attention. She thrust open doors with a wide, swinging gesture, before her glasses appeared with mirage-like suddenness. The white overall followed several seconds later.

'Good morning, Mr Hanse.'

'Good morning, Miss Beak.'

'And how are we today, Mr Hanse.'

'Very well, Miss Beak. And yourself?'

'Very good, too, Mr Hanse. Beautiful day.'

'Yes. Beautiful.'

'Jolly beautiful, I should say.'

'I should say.'

'Good morning, Miss Calne.'

'Good morning, Miss Beak . . .'

It was the same every day. The verbal routine ensured that Miss Beak could keep her distance from these lesser beings. Mostly she avoided Christian names with staff, believing that in using them, her authority would be diminished in their eyes. She would not say good morning to that rude Mr Young in the History department though. She had greeted him at the end of last term (not everyone would have bothered first thing in the morning) and he had been most offensive:

Hello Hello Miss Beak
And how are you today?
You're looking very well,
Hooray Hooray Hooray.

Most rude. He was probably drunk. She'd heard from Mrs Bowles' son in Form Three that he was an alcoholic and that he kept a bottle of whisky in his stock-room. First thing in the morning as well. Disgusting.

Miss Beak strained her words to the point of excessive politeness. Continued practice had made them sound as if this were her normal way of speaking. Through pursed lips, she affected an accent of clipped efficiency as her hands flicked switches, flew from jars to cupboards, sinks to ceilings. If someone pressed the wrong button on a machine when she wasn't looking, she knew instinctively, as if they had touched the hem of her garment and were now drawing on her superior knowledge and power. Then she would appear as if from nowhere and come to their aid.

Teachers' resources came under her exclusive jurisdiction. She kept a large hard-backed red book, in which she logged the names of staff who had used more than their quota of paper, tapes and materials during the course of the term. A register of their Demands Made and Requests Granted went into a black book. Interest was at the rate of 10% p.a. and staff were quick to regret their overdrafts when Miss Beak enforced a temporary ban on their paper supplies. Sometimes it was a whole term before the suspension was lifted.

Graystone waited in the empty room. He could not understand why it had been left unlocked. He thought, scratched his mole and decided to risk taking the paper he needed, without asking permission. After all, it was only a few sheets he needed to try out the machine. He bent to the lowest cupboard where he knew the paper was kept. It was padlocked.

'Naughty, Naughty, Mr Harold.' A voice boomed magically through the air; then came a pair of glasses, and finally the white overall of Miss Beak materialised from behind the tallest cupboard.

'I . . . uh . . . just wanted a couple of sheets to try out on the

79

photocopier.' Graystone shrank like a guilty schoolboy back against the wall.

'Well, we don't come in and help ourselves, do we now?' Miss Beak laid her hand on the sleeve of Graystone's jacket. She peered over the top of her glasses and shook her forefinger. 'But I'll tell you what I'll do.' She pulled Graystone aside confidentially, as if about to impart a great secret. She stroked his sleeve with two fingers, glanced suspiciously over her shoulder and decided it would be safer if she shut the door. Then she took him by the elbow, giving him a gentle, reassuring squeeze, should he fear he was still in disgrace. He stood speechless.

'I'll tell you what I'll do,' repeated Miss Beak. 'I'll lend you – only lend, mind you – some of Miss Lyle's. New teachers never like to use their full quota. But . . . and this is a big But . . . You must pay her back!' She pinched the skin on Graystone's hand, a gesture of playful rebuke. He yelped.

Miss Beak stood on a chair and removed a tin from the top of the cupboard. Inside was a small key. She stepped down and put the key in the padlock. She turned it slowly, as she might do the dial of a safe. It clicked. The stiff metal loop of the padlock came away. Miss Beak unhooked it from the cupboard. She opened the doors. The moment never failed to have the quality of revelation for her. Stiff brown packets were piled neatly erect like building bricks; plastic wrappers caught the light; fresh white sheets glowed in the dark; coloured sheets – yellow, blue and green – mingled like the layers of a marble cake. There was paper of such shapes and sizes as Graystone had never seen before. He crouched at Miss Beak's side, admiring the display. He grew conscious of his sleeve brushing against her starched white overall, herself a pack of crisp white paper waiting to be unwrapped and fanned into loose sheets by expert fingers.

'Here you are.' She handed him a small pile of A4 plain white paper. Graystone's mouth reflected grievous disappointment.

'We'll see, Mr Harold, we'll see.' Miss Beak gave a knowing wink. Graystone smiled, a little boy accepting a small lollipop as a preliminary to a large bag of toffees. He straightened the edges of his meagre loot and left the den. I know just how to handle people, he thought.

Miss Beak waited until the door was closed before she

replaced the key in its tin. She heard Graystone's footsteps recede and this time hid the tin in the cupboard next to the window. I know just how to handle people, she thought.

A group of semi-interested teachers gathered for the first performance of the photocopier, arranged for 10.40 a.m. Liz Caversham, dangling a rose-hip tea-bag into a mug of hot water, hopped excitedly from one leg to the other, offering advice; Gareth Watts, head of Craft, prodded various dials, much to Graystone's annoyance; and Marcus Brent, head of Music, was breathing heavily down the back of his wind specialist. Many, bored by the delay, retired to make coffee. Graystone eyed his steadily dwindling audience, coughed, paused and affected nonchalance, as he would with an unsettled class of children. The little speech he was about to make was 'essential to the ears of all those with an aspiration to using the machine.'

'Ladies and gentlemen,' he began (someone else slipped out from the back row), 'it seems that Mother Necessity forces us into the position of having to warm the machine well in advance of its being used. Nevertheless, it is sufficiently warm at this moment in time for you to witness a little demonstration with regard to procuring the production of your own copies.'

Graystone elucidated the detailed instructions and waved his hands appropriately with reference to particular parts of the machine. He exposed a sheet of paper to the front row, as if inviting them to inspect it for evidence of trickery, and commenced the performance. He laid the paper in the cartridge and thrust it into the side of the machine with the force of a steel blade, knowing that the victim inside would remain unharmed. It was the show of a magician, presenting his material according to a craft of which the audience remains ignorant. He was an artist. He laid the palm of his hand against the side where a whirring could be heard. A gentle throbbing tickled his hand; warmth sank into his fingertips. Slowly, carefully, he lined up a copy of his Tunnel poems, opened at the centre pages, within the A4 markers on the glass panel of the machine. He replaced the red flap and smoothed it with gentle, caressing movements. His last stroke had the finality of sealing a lid on a coffin.

'READY' shone in luminous green; 'H' signified a medium-

81

dark print; the number '1' was selected on the 'COPIES' dial. All was prepared for the first showing, the preview of greater things to come. Graystone's magic finger pressed an orange button. The whirring intestines sounded. His hand awaited their offspring. But alas! The machine groaned and the whirring died; 'CHECK' appeared in red.

'Hm,' muttered Graystone, humiliated. 'Hm, now, let me see . . .' Several spectators took advantage of the delay as a means of retreat. 'Ha! Got it!' The remedy administered – the removal of a piece of jammed paper – allowed the show to go on. Foreplay commenced again. The cartridge was re-loaded, less heavily, and inserted. 'Ah,' came a satisfied growl. 'Wait . . . turn it off. . . wait . . . on again . . . press green button . . . draw blank with red and green lights together . . . ready again on green . . . Easy.'

Graystone muttered on to the single remaining witness, Miss Lyle. He pressed the orange button again. There was a click, a rumble, a bright flashing light and a white, ejaculatory spread in the tray. The first copy echoed its arrival in the otherwise empty room.

Breeding and Birth

Stallions have no special mating season and are always ready to mate. The whole process takes place over six stages:-

1. *Visual appraisal of the mare; physical nuzzles around the flanks and hind quarters.*
2. *Mounting.*
3. *Intromission (Entering the Mare). The stallion should not be restrained too long before being allowed to mount, as the glans sometimes increase in size before intromission.*
4. *Pelvic thrusts, the stallion maintaining his grip and balance with his forelimbs. In many cases, he grasps the mare around the withers or the lower part of the neck with his teeth. This can be dangerous, and a gripping-pad should be placed around the neck of the mare.*
5. *Ejaculation, often accompanied by flagging tail. With some horses, it is difficult to assess whether ejaculation has taken place. In these circumstances, feel for the pulse wave which passes along the urethra*

82

*on the lower border of the penis. Utmost care must be taken, as some
animals resent being handled at this stage.*

*Foaling is normally a straightforward process. The new foal will learn
to eat by imitating its mother, but as the mother's supply of milk
decreases, the foal should spend time with another young companion.
To gain the foal's confidence, always show fairness and deserved
correction, otherwise sullenness and bad temper will result.*

Losing a Foal

By the middle of the second term, Timothy Leach had
mastered his school tie. He also found that his father had been
right, after all: he did enjoy school. Chemistry was one of the
most enjoyable subjects, and last week they had filled the whole
laboratory with white fluff after an experiment with metafuel.
But he liked Art most of all. At the moment, he was making a
fruit basket out of straw. He had started with a flat wooden
base, on which Mr Allen had set the first straws so that they
stood upright in long tufts. The rest was left to him. You had to
wet each long straw first, to prevent it from snapping when it
was wound onto the frame. The end had to be tucked inside, to
let the best side face outwards. Timothy liked basket-making
because he was the only one in the class who wanted to do it. He
could help himself to straw and water, without worrying that
someone else would come along and make a mess of it. That
was what he hated about painting. Half the lesson was spent in
cleaning the mixing trays and brushes that the previous class
had left dirty; then you had to share paints with about three
other people, all of whom appeared to be colour-blind. Browns,
greens and reds soon became indistinguishable from one
another, and hardly anyone stuck to their own jar of water. But
seated on a chair by the window, his shirt sleeves rolled up,
Timothy knew that each long piece of cool, crisp white straw
belonged only to him. He was always the last to pack away, and
when the home-time bell rang and he finally went out into the
yard, he always had to blink his way back into consciousness,
readjusting his eyes to the real world like he did when leaving
the cinema in daylight.

Today, it was warm. His grey winter trousers were too hot on days like this, and the strong sun outside made him blink more than usual. As he reached the school gate, he remembered that he had left his sandwich-box in his form room. There was still one chocolate biscuit left in it – but no, he would not go back for it now. He was frightened being inside the school when everyone else was leaving. Last term, he had waited in Mr Graystone's study because he had missed the bus home. There was no sound but the ticking of a large old clock on the wall. Everything seemed bigger in there: the clock, the chairs, the paperweight on the desk. It was hard to imagine voices in the room: as if every object forbade you to talk in its presence. Timothy had recently seen a film about a shrinking man, and sitting on the huge chair, felt sure that he too was slipping away. Every tick of the clock seemed to chip off a little more of him. He would have to get away before he disappeared completely. He left the room and ran down the long corridor that led to his classroom. But it had gone. It did not appear around the next corner either. Now there was a green wall, then a yellow, and parts of the school he had never seen before. And he ran and ran and ran, too frightened to cry, until a man caught him and he screamed. Too confused to see his face, he waved his fists in the air, hitting out with no direction and uncertain of purpose. Ssh, ssh, he heard the voice say. Tim. Tim. And somehow the sound of his name quieted him; as if, for a brief second, it was his own self that was holding him. Tim. Tim. It's all right. It's only me. Dad.

The chocolate biscuit would keep. It would give him something to look forward to in the morning. Maybe he would try to eat it in class. In Maths, perhaps. Mr Anderson didn't worry much about that sort of thing, as he was always eating in class anyway. Whenever his desk lid went up and he disappeared completely behind it, you could hear the rustle of sweet papers. Everyone pretended they noticed nothing, but when he came round the class to help out with problems, they caught the sugary smell of barley sugar on his breath. Occasionally, he experimented with aniseed or mints, but it was the barley sugar to which he returned: hard, orange cubes, wrapped in golden cellophane, coating his teeth as surely as if he had been a heavy smoker.

Timothy waited outside the school gates in what was, by now, a familiar queue. He had even made friends with pupils he had met just standing at the stop. But today, none of them were there, and Timothy took out his French vocabulary book to start revising for the weekly test. '*Le bifteck,*' he said aloud. 'Steak. *La boisson.* Drink. *Le camarade.* Friend. *Un autobus.* Bus. *Un autobus.* Bus. *Un autobus.*'

Afterwards, they asked pupils to try and recall the exact sequence of events, but most were too shocked even to speak. One remembered seeing the bus coming quickly down the hill; another thought he saw a green car on the wrong side of the road; the teacher on duty said that he heard only the screeching of brakes – but afterwards thought the noise may have been inside his head. The police went straight away to the home of Timothy Leach. There was a knock on the door. And that was that.

The church was full. Andrew Young, Timothy's form teacher, spoke of him as a quiet boy, hard-working and polite. There was a wreath from the form, one from each year group and one from the staff. Grief was allocated proportionate to the time and space this short life had occupied in other people's routines. Timothy Leach was deleted from mark-books and registers; text books and library books were returned and his desk was emptied. Badges, raffle-tickets and money, a theatre ticket and a school clarinet each went back for redistribution.

Almost everything, in the end, was on loan; there seemed so much life to give back, and yet, by the same token, so much it was almost impossible to receive: a half-finished straw basket, a painting barely dry, and an essay marked C+, the teacher's comment in large, bold letters at the foot of the page: 'Ending unoriginal.' Timothy Leach had covered six sides of foolscap with an essay titled 'Journey Into Space'. The final sentence read: 'And then I woke up and discovered it had all been a dream.'

Parenting

The Christmas mock 'O', 'A' Levels and C.S.E.s were over, and thus for many the struggle with authority was coming to a close. Examination papers had been secured in bundles, and they travelled home with the staff, cramped amongst Christmas trees and presents, to be marked. The temptation to mark pupils down because of class behaviour or simply an ugly face had, for the most part, been resisted. Similarly, though more difficult to stop, had been the temptation to mark pupils up because of parents who were known troublemakers – usually those who were teachers themselves. The system operated for the mutual benefit of all; such corruption, as they were all aware, would only upset the cohesiveness of such a complex structure. In the second week of the Spring Term, the parents –first those of Form Five – were therefore invited to come to Riverside and pay what was, for many, their last respects to Parents' Evenings.

It was not without a touch of sadness that many drove through the yellow iron gates for the last time that January evening. Five years earlier – though it seemed like only yesterday (not, however, for Alan Jennings' father, whose operation had cost him the time-keeping half of his brain) – they had been coming to ponder the careers of their twelve-year-old darlings. Little had some of them contemplated, during the tender years, the green hair or shaved heads of their saplings; and little had others thought that the child to whom they had given several black eyes would turn out quite so well. There were many faces watching the mirror that night as they dressed for the last meeting. Many faces searching for the years that had slipped, unforeseeably, through the looking-glass.

There were always many practical considerations to be worked out to ensure the smooth running of school meetings. For this particular one, Graystone had been appointed Chief Co-ordinator and he set about his duties with the usual alacrity. With funds from Resources (Miss Beak had really taken quite a shine to him), he purchased an enormous sheet of white paper from the Art department ('I'd give it to you, Harold, but you know, our resources will inevitably be cut back as a result of the photocopier,' said Peter Allen).

He drew up hundreds of perfect squares on the main body of the sheet, leaving a column at the side for teachers' names and their assigned rooms which he entered in block capitals. In the top row of squares, he printed 6.00 p.m.–8.00 p.m., at five minute intervals. Finally, the names of the parents were listed, according to the times they had requested on the statutory letter. Graystone smiled with proud satisfaction as he stood back to survey his work on the notice-board. It was the same look that had first irradiated his face when he admired The Gainsborough Lady. But this was no time for self-praise. There was the squash and coffee to be organized, the biscuits to buy. Should he buy custard creams or Bourbon? The Jaffa cakes at the First Form 'Welcome' evening had just about broken the Sundries fund and then it had been so difficult to keep a check on those who tried to steal a second. One chocolate, one plain, Graystone had always been taught, and he intended that others should be made to follow suit. Maybe he should opt for something simpler altogether. Rich Tea, perhaps. Garibaldi. He would ask Matron for her advice.

'Hmph! Why are we always in the cold rooms?' asked Ellen Ridgeway.

Others gathered around Graystone's masterpiece.

'Well *I'm* not staying until eight o'clock.'

'Nor me.'

'Some of us have to. I've got twenty-three coming to see me.'

'Sign of a bad teacher.'

'Or an exceptionally good one.'

'Damn – the Bells are coming first. That should put me in a good mood!'

'The psychopathic father?'

'And daughter, if you ask me.'

Roy Dixon appeared with a clipboard. 'Has anyone . . . where's . . . oh dear, oh no . . .' and disappeared.

'Raymond is a lazy little sod who has no chance of passing anything but water. So don't give me exams, I know all about those – eight "O" Levels, three "A" Levels, a degree *and* a teaching certificate just to get this far – so don't go blaming the whole damn system on me. I'm just doing my job and if you ask me, your son . . .' Jonathan Hayward breaks off quickly and makes hasty adjustments to his mental script as the first parents approach his desk.

The couple look nervous and Hayward is encouraged. He

thrusts out a confident hand towards the mother. She is exceptionally tall, the height that devours with mere presence. Hayward sits again. The husband is totally bald and much smaller – absurdly so. Hayward tries to catch his good eye but is unconsciously drawn to the one three times its size, the ball of which is travelling like a moving bull's eye target towards his nose. Hayward relaxes into his managerial role, the couple fitting the bill of a holiday camp duo coming for an audition. A gentle pair.

'Our Raymond – he's staying on for 'A' Level,' demands the mother. (Hayward has been mistaken.) 'He's not leaving . . . English is very important . . . We want him to be a barrister, don't we?' She prods her husband sharply on the arm. 'I said, Don't we?' He topples on his chair and nods acquiescently: a dummy that has not yet learnt the art of accompanying the ventriloquist's voice with facial expressions.

Hayward shrinks in his chair as the woman's mouth gapes more widely and he is bombed with spittle. 'Well, let's . . .' he attempts tentatively, raising a subtle hand to wipe away her liquid venom.

' "A" Level or nothing.' Her final statement on the matter.

Stationed around the room is the rest of the English department: Steven Hall, Patricia White and James McGill, each seated defensively in a corner, blocked in by two wooden desks and two empty chairs opposite.

'Can I help you?' says James McGill to a lost couple.

'Mr Hall?'

McGill indicates Hall in the opposite corner and the couple are passed along like a 'Happy Families' playing card.

'Hello, Mr and Mrs . . . ?' asks Hall, standing to shake hands. The woman's grip wrenches his hand. The joints click.

'Thomas.'

'Mr and Mrs Thomas, take a seat, please,' They sit. 'I . . . uh . . . don't seem to have the surname Thomas in my markbook.'

'Thomas Kale,' says the mother, firmly. 'Five "T".'

'Oh, I see. Thomas is his first name.' (Why the hell didn't you say so, then?) 'Kale . . . Kale . . .' Hall flicks through the Fifth Form set of 'O' Level papers. 'Ah, yes. 15% for Literature and 29% for Language. I'm afraid I don't think Thomas has worked as hard as he might have for these exams. But if he pulls his socks up, a lot can happen between now and Easter.'

'But he'll be doing 'O' Level?'

'Well, I think perhaps he'd be better able to cope with the C.S.E. In all honesty, I think Thomas finds it difficult to express himself in the conventional modes of language required by the 'O' Level.' (He's monosyllabic, thinks Hall.)

'That's exactly what his father says.'

'I do not.'

'You're always putting him down.'

'I am not.'

'Uh . . . uh . . .' attempts a pacifying Hall. 'You see, the C.S.E. is, in fact, quite a useful exam.'

'About as useful as a Sociology degree,' says Dad.

'And what's wrong with a Sociology degree?' retaliates Mum, an Open University Sociology graduate.

'She had awful trouble with that sonnet you asked her to write,' Mrs Payton is saying to Patricia White. 'I'd like to see her doing more comprehensions.'

'Well, actually, she did very well with the sonnet. I think I gave her a B+.' Patricia checks her mark-book.

'And we're not keen on all this literature lark,' adds the father. 'It's just storing facts, if you ask me, like history; no use to you in the real world. I don't want our Carol to become a dreamer.'

'You don't look old enough to be Tracey's mother,' smiles Hayward at the blossoming Mrs Wheedon.

'Well, I'm not, actually,' she blushes. 'It's his second marriage and I . . . uh . . . we . . .'

'Oh.'

'And when we go on long journeys, I make him play spelling games the whole way,' says Mrs Bolton to James McGill.

'Andrew thinks you don't like him,' says Mr Bolton.

'Nonsense,' says McGill, lying.

'I mean, English is so important,' says Mrs Weekes.

'I know that or I wouldn't be teaching it,' snaps Hall.

'Tell her we're going to write a Miltonic epic next week,' says Patricia, spitefully.

'I didn't realize,' says Hayward.

'You see, when I met John – that is, Tracey's father – my ex-

89

husband . . . comforted, I suppose you could say, Eleanor – that's Tracey's real mother – and married her. Belinda – that's my real daughter, the eldest – is with her father. I've kept Tim, and then Eleanor and Frank – that's my ex-husband – have also got Kevin and Lucy – that's Eleanor and John's other two.'

'I see,' says Hayward.

Out of room one, up the first set of stairs and into the Science complex. The small menagerie squeaks at the presence of strangers. There is a smell of sawdust and small life. This is the area where the remedial pupils are disposed of when teachers consider that their brains have soaked up sufficient information for the day. In the blue cage is the longest resident, a hamster, caught by its front teeth on the top rung of its climbing-frame. The body wriggles, the frantic claws scrape helplessly at the air. The black eyes dilate; the small white teeth stretch from pink, expanding gums, as the body pulls a little more on its own weight. Suddenly, the creature drops to safety and we can, with clear minds, enter the first Science laboratory.

The Chemistry and Physics members of the Science department are positioned behind gas-taps, should any parents prove difficult. Alan Richards, the overall head of Science, is at the front; Jill Bates, Chemistry, and John Deignton and Nigel Wilton, Physics, are seated in alternate rows.

Jill Bates watches Mr Earling's nostrils which gape with the rhythm of his breathing like a pair of gills. Suddenly there is a cup of coffee and a ginger nut on the bench, and the teacher is glad of the diversion. She sinks her teeth into the biscuit and Mrs Ealing looks at her husband with a See-I-told-you-that's-all-they-do-anyway expression.

He ignores her. 'I don't know how the pupils manage to concentrate with such attractive teachers in the classroom,' smiles the sycophant.

'Thank you,' says Jill, choking and sending a soggy lump of aerobic phlegm over to Mrs Ealing's blouse.

'Come along, Gerald,' she scowls. 'Hmph! They didn't have kids teaching when I was at school,' is intended for the teacher's ears as the couple walks away.

John Deignton wonders how he can prevent Mrs Kohl from spilling out over his desk, where her buttons have come undone.

'My dorr – ht – er . . . She think you won – derr – ful! You ex – cell – ent teacher.'

Deignton smiles. He knows.

'Well, in all confidence . . .' hisses Nigel Wilton into an ear. 'I don't think the teacher before me was all that helpful.'

'Pardon?'

'Mrs – Rogers – last – year – not – helpful,' he says, more emphatically and with a vigorous shake of his head.

'I didn't quite . . .'

'YOUR SON'S TEACHER – A MORON!'

'Oh.'

'She's not very well behaved,' says John Deignton, to a surprised mother. 'I've had to move her to a different seat, she doesn't do her homework, she's easily distracted in class . . . Why, only yesterday . . .'

Blank faces opposite. Recognition spreads across Deignton's face. Shit, wrong child. 'Mind you, she's been a lot better today.'

In the Art room sits Peter Allen.

'The problem is, Jane has missed so much work. I know she's been unwell, but she has hardly anything in her folder.'

Jane Sanders' mother exhales confidential breath towards him and leans across the table. 'But you see, there are a lot of *personal* difficulties.' She winks. 'Can't be helped.'

'I see. Well, as I said . . .'

'Her womb.' She delivers the statement in a voice the Angel Gabriel might have used on unsuspecting virgins. Her husband conveniently finds a tree outside on which to focus his attention. 'P.P.T.' (Pre-period tension? Post-prandial tapeworms? muses Allen.) 'They want to scrape her.'

'Well, I'm willing to . . .'

'But there are problems.' Another wink. 'You see, she's still a virgin,' she announces ceremoniously.

'Oh.'

'But it's giving her a lot of worry. We're Mormons, you see. And the condition could worsen unless something's done about it. So what do you suggest?'

Mr Sanders squashes his head a little deeper into his collar.

*

91

'Good evening, Headmaster,' said Graystone. 'I was just saying to Mr Swainson here, every beetle is a gazelle in the eyes of its mother.'

'I'm sorry?' said Salmon.

'Just an old proverb, Headmaster.'

'Please, call me Ken,' said the Headmaster.

Graystone blushed. Mr Swainson nibbled on a ginger nut.

The Home Economics room was now filling with parents who were taking a half-time break from the ordeal of teacher confrontation. It was now the turn of the senior staff to sell the more general aspects of school life. Graystone had memorised several new quotations – some golden oldies which always went down well, in addition to a number of topical ones, just to show that at Riverside, contact with the outside world was maintained. The sexless presence of Grace Calne ensured that parents stayed away from the topic of youth and immorality, while Roy Dixon assured anxious parents that the school's overall policy with regard to timetable choices was in the most capable of hands. It was the task of Kenneth Salmon to mingle with the crowd like Christ, giving parents who could not get close enough to converse, the opportunity of touching the hem of his jacket.

'Good evening, Mr Salmon,' said Mrs Howells. 'How are you?'

Salmon watched the movement of her lips, without comprehension. It was as if the words had fallen out of their sentence and dropped to the floor. He would have to gather them up and put them back together before they could again make sense.

'A lot here tonight,' said Mrs Howells.

Catch! his father had called, but he always dropped the ball. Mrs Howells' words slipped as easily from his mind. It seemed minutes before he located the sounds: A-lot-here-tonight; and then further minutes, while he sifted through the jumble of words in his own mind, wrapping his answer up into a neat sentence to send back.

'Yes. A good turnout,' he said, watching the words run like drops along a wire.

And still she talked on. Mrs Howells. Words pouring from her thin, pink lips, small change from a one-armed bandit. He heard it rattle as it hit the floor, too much now to collect in one

92

small purse. He let the words alone in a heap of conversation at his feet.

Mrs Howells. Mrs Grange. Mr Leaman. Mr and Mrs Smith. The second Mrs Harris. He waded from one parent to another through the fall of sounds, each more indistinguishable than the last. For a minute he was able to pick up the pieces of sentences and make a shape to which he could respond. But then his own words too began to fall. He was playing with two balls: catch, throw, catch, throw; and the two balls bounced to the ground. Butterfingers! his father had called.

'Well, I mean, you know, every beetle is a gazelle in the eyes of its mother.' Graystone had grown quite partial to the analogy and had succeeded in cornering another unsuspecting parent.

'Is the Headmaster ... uh ... all right, Mr Graystone?' asked Mrs Samuels.

'Just a little tired, I expect,' he answered.

'He doesn't look at all well.'

'Stresses and strains of the job. You know, as Shakespeare says ...'

Mrs Samuels smuggled another ginger nut out from under Graystone's guard.

'How did you find that Mr Hall?' said Mrs Willis to Mrs Stokes.

'First turning on the left,' said Mr Stokes.

'Shut up, George,' said Mrs Stokes.

'I don't like his hair,' said Mrs Willis.

'He's not married either,' said Mrs Stokes.

'Suspicious that – for a man his age,' said Mr Willis.

'Wise devil,' said Mr Stokes.

'George – I told you to shut up,' said Mrs Stokes.

And George shuts up.

Kenneth Salmon left the Home Economics block and made his way across the yard to the main part of the school. It was on occasions like this that his office might prove a temptation to prowlers. But it was safe. Dark and deserted. He unlocked the door and crept in, but did not turn on the light. He emptied his pockets and spread the contents over his desk: a brand new pair of tiny pliers, a length of fuse wire and several strips of copper. Outside, it had started to rain. For an instant, a sheet of lightning illuminated the toys on his desk and the room shone like Christmas morning. Then, thunder. And finally, rain. Rain that fell like the tiny drops of words he had tried to send along the wire; washed over the bed of coins until their chatter could no longer be heard. Rain that flooded the sounds around his feet and carried them away, far away, to a distant sea.

'Geoff! Geoff!' called James McGill across the JCR. 'I've been looking for you everywhere. Can I have a word, please?'

'Sure.' Geoff Symms followed him to the window.

'Look, I know it's not my place . . .' McGill glanced confidentially over his shoulder, '. . . but . . . well, it's about Phil.'

'Oh?'

'He's been acting rather strangely.'

'Really?'

'This morning . . . it was after registration. I was teaching in room four and I realized Form Five's books were still down here, so I left the class and came down.' Another glance, this time over the other shoulder. 'Anyway, he was in here.'

'So?'

'Reading.'

'Reading?'

'Reading a newspaper. Anyway, as I came in, he put it down very quickly. And . . . you won't like this, Geoff . . . it was *The Guardian.*'

Symms laughed aloud. 'Very funny.'

'Look, Geoff – I'm serious.'

'Listen, Jim. No member of my department would wipe his arse with *The Guardian.* He wouldn't be in my department if he did.'

'No, no. Taylor. Phil Taylor. The chairman. *Our* chairman.'

Symms swallowed his smile. The colour of his normally red face drained suddenly to his neck. Slowly, it started to rise again and stopped just short of his cheekbones. He let out a growl. 'W - h - a - a - t?' He screwed up his eyes and spittle ran down his chin. 'Are you sure?'

94

'Absolutely sure. I'd know that paper with my eyes shut.'

'I don't suppose there's any chance you were . . .'

'No chance at all, I'm sorry. And I heard from Andrew Gray's father last night – he buys a copy from their shop on Saturday mornings.'

Symms gulped his coffee. 'This is serious.'

'I just thought you should know.' McGill had achieved his desired response. 'You know . . . after all our work . . .' he added, squeezing Symms' arm. 'Anything I can do.'

'Of course, of course,' said Symms, distracted.

For a small subscription fee, members of the JCR newspaper syndicate were permitted to read, and complete the crosswords of *The Daily Telegraph, The Guardian* and, on Fridays, *The Times Educational Supplement*. Since its founding five years previously, the syndicate had been governed by a right-wing leadership. Symms had campaigned assiduously to bring this about, and although he had only been runner-up to Taylor in the last election, he was at least glad that the syndicate had not passed over into the hands of the other party. Now he shuddered at the prospect of change. McGill had always hated Taylor and felt that Symms was by far the stronger candidate; he relished the fact that if Symms were to take over the leadership as a result of this split, he, as chief campaigner, would be well placed to receive favours from above: spare dinner tickets, the occasional lifting of a supervision, the extraction of a rowdy pupil from his class. Yes, he had made the right decision in approaching Symms first.

Symms had difficulty in concentrating during the remainder of the morning's lessons. If Taylor *was* turning pink, then something should be done about it quickly; things like this tended to be catching. He decided upon a strategy. He would start to collate evidence against Taylor which, if proven, would constitute moves towards the holding of another election for the leadership. He started with his own department.

Philip Lissold was in the main Geography room, fondling a large globe. His left hand caressed the underbelly of Australia; his right finger poked itself up the Orinoco.

'Phil – look, I've heard some rather disturbing news this morning.'

'Not your father . . .?'

'Worse. It's about Phil Taylor.'

'Mm?' Lissold slid each of his hands towards a pole.

'Jim told me he saw him reading *The Guardian* this morning.'

'Shit!' Lissold clutched the equator. He would not even eat chips from any paper but the *Telegraph*, though many had said that he was only after a Scale 2 and therefore trying to cultivate popularity in the right places. 'That's bad.'

'I know. But look, keep it quiet for a while. Just until we're certain.'

Symms left the room just in time to see an eavesdropper turn the corner at the end of the corridor. By mid-afternoon, all speculation and rumour had to be confirmed: the evidence weighed heavily against Taylor. Not only had he been witnessed reading *The Guardian* on several occasions (and one person's evidence dating as far back as November of the previous term), but he had probably raised the cost of members' subscriptions in order to buy his own *Guardian* from Mr Gray on Saturdays. By the end of the day, further incriminating evidence had been stacked against him.

'I'll tell you something else,' said Liz Caversham, 'keep it to yourself, though. He and Pat are *very friendly*, if you know what I mean.'

So that was it: the switching of Taylor's reading matter was the final confirmation of his affair with Patricia White; the affair, confirmation of the treason. Someone else remembered someone else saying that Taylor had said to some other person that newspapers came second only to sex. It was thereby established that Taylor had clearly been presented with an ultimatum: Patricia and *The Guardian*, or no Patricia and the *Telegraph*. The spirit had proved willing, but the flesh was indeed weak.

It was also discovered that the system, under its present leader, was considerably more lax than it appeared to be on the surface. Symms, upon asking for the official list of members, discovered, much to his dismay, that no such list had ever been compiled. It had always been left to long-standing members to store the list on memory and then to prevent non-members, or non-paid-up members, from touching (as if with an intention to read), or actually reading, the papers. Many, however, had

96

been less than fastidious in the carrying out of their duties, and the system had thereby been laid open to corruption.

Richard Smith, the classicist of the SCR, benefited most from the laxity of the system. Refusing to pay a subscription fee, as he was only an occasional visitor to the JCR, he had no intention of paying for the pleasures of permanent residents. He therefore devised intricate plots by which he might acquire the *News of the World* free of charge.

Most successful was the Post-Registration scheme. After marking 4A's register, he went across to the JCR under the guise of friendliness towards his colleagues. When he had made enough desultory conversation to make his presence seem a natural occurrence (even desired, he flattered himself), he sidled towards the table where the papers lay neatly folded: his favourite was *The Guardian* because he preferred the typeface. He shuffled sideways, one foot chasing, the other in retreat, the like poles of two magnets. As an added subtlety, he kept a conversation going at the same time: his head facing those he addressed while his right hand, a pawn moving quietly, one square at a time, carried out the deed. As soon as he thought all attention was off him (it invariably was), he grasped the paper in his fist. Its weight was slowly transferred to both hands, and clutching it below elbow level, he allowed his fingers the experience of a long and pleasurable sniff before raising the contents to his eyes to be devoured. Then, having acclimatised themselves to the cold, crisp surface, his fingers started to unfold the package. He affected disinterest as his eyes skimmed the front page: this allowed him the 'It-wasn't-worth-reading-anyhow' let-out, should he be caught in the act. He never was. The first glance was like a pre-dinner glass of sherry: enjoyable in itself, but also the foretaste to something more palatable. Smith gulped in the headlines; then, as he relaxed unnoticed, allowed himself sips of smaller print. Always he succeeded in finishing the whole glass. Then he smiled, licked the corners of his wet mouth and walked nonchalantly away.

Symms closed the dossier on Taylor's case. Something would most certainly have to be done.

97

'Armoured Crispy Shoulders' rose feebly on the air like the last dying voices from the trenches. The cheeks of Hilary Williams, full rounded bellows, winded her trumpet to the extent that it was the only instrument to be heard in the orchestra. Marcus Brent, conducting, waved his arms in a frantic attempt to whip up the other instruments.

Graystone stepped to the front of the stage and leaned forward, his right ear angled in an attempt to catch the precise words of the hymn. He raised his hand to Brent, who slapped the air with his baton.

'Just one moment, please, Mr Brent. I don't believe everyone's singing. We'll try it again, please. Remember that this is a hymn of great strength and joy in Christian fellowship, soldiers and brothers marching forward together to victory in Christ's name. You're sounding like a pack of deserters. Now let's hear it again – with a bit of feeling this time. Thank you, Mr Brent.'

Brent began conducting again, this time faster in the hope that tempo might improve voice.

'J . . . just a moment . . .' Graystone stepped forward again. Hilary Williams burped; Brent's baton sighed through the air. 'Form One boys seem to think they're not included; so we'll have the first verse again, this time with Form One boys only. Thank you, Mr Brent.'

This time, the Christian soldiers positively galloped to their war, and the hymn happily reached its conclusion with no further interruption. At its close, Nigel Simpkin, a prefect and the morning's reader, stepped forward and stood behind the lectern. He was feeling rather annoyed at having been asked to change the reading at such short notice and nervously crumpled Reverend Rock's note in his pocket as he opened the large school Bible.

'This morning's reading . . .'

There were several snorts from the pupils gathered for assembly. The school took great delight in hearing prefects' voices. Simpkin's had a soft and slow melodious ring to it; his head of tight blond curls contributed to his rather effeminate manner. 'Oooh' and giggles bubbled in the middle of the hall from those pupils hidden from teachers patrolling the end of lines. Some accompanied their comments by placing a hand on their hips and making teapot wrists. Graystone saw two pink spots of embarrassment appear beneath the boy's eyes, but decided against another admonishment which, he felt, would only confuse Simpkin further. Gradually, the noise died down.

'This morning's reading is taken from . . .' The words became big and blurred as Simpkin stared down with watery eyes. '. . . is taken from The Song of Songs, chapter 5, verses 10–16.' Reverend Rock, standing at the rear of the stage, frowned and rummaged for his list of the week's readings.

> ' "My lover is handsome and strong;
> he is one of ten thousand." '

Muffled laughter came from Form Six, standing at the back of the hall.

> ' "His face is bronzed and smooth;
> his hair is wavy,
> black as raven." '

Simpkin's voice dropped. He pulled at a curl and twisted it round his fingers. Coughs and choking sounds spluttered towards the floor from hanging Sixth Form heads, shaking with uncontrollable laughter.

The words of verse 12 merged into one large inkspot. Simpkin blinked; a tear fell and blistered the page; the words were once again in focus. His right hand clenched the note in his pocket.

> ' "His eyes are as beautiful as doves by
> a flowing brook,
> doves washed in milk and standing
> by the stream.
> His cheeks . . ." '

Graystone's eyes left the back of the reader and followed the line of boys at the back of the hall from left to right: Stephen Wallis, Alan Regan, Simon Henley . . . Which one was to blame? How he disliked their red faces, bloated with laughter.

    ' "His cheeks are as lovely as a garden
          that is full of herbs and spices.
    His lips are like lilies,
          wet with liquid myrrh." '

Simpkin wiped his mouth where two estuaries of tears had gathered at the corners. He felt no anger or hate now. He wrapped his fingers tightly around the note. He would reach the end.

    ' "His hands are well-formed,
          and he wears rings set with gems." '

He must reach the end, Graystone thought. He fixed his eyes on the back of Simpkin's head, willing him on.

    ' "His body . . . his *body*. . ." '

Simpkin raised his voice.

    ' ". . . is like *smooth* ivory,
          with sapphires set in it." '

They were only words, after all.

    ' "His *thighs* . . ." '

Alan Regan now looked epileptic. Graystone was sure he was the chief culprit.

    ' "His th - igh - s,' said Simpkin, softly,
      ' "are columns of alabaster
        set in sockets of gold" '

The row of Sixth Formers began to shift uneasily from one foot to the other.

    ' "He is . . . ma - jes - tic, like the Lebanon Mountains
          with their towering cedars.
    His mouth . . . is sweet to kiss;

everything . . . *everything* about him enchants me. This is what my lover is like . . ." '

Simpkin raised his eyes to the back row. The Sixth Form were still.

' "*This* is what my lover is like,
women of Jerusalem." '

He continued to stare. His eyes had cleared. It was as if someone had polished the edges of each individual figure in the back row.

'Here endeth the lesson,' he said, and closed the Bible.

'Let us pray, let us pray,' said Reverend Rock, rushing to the lectern.

Simpkin stepped aside and resumed his place on the stage. Graystone squeezed his arm.

'Now where did I put that prayer?' The Reverend rummaged through his pockets. Oh well, better make it up. 'Oh Lord, we pray this morning for all those who are less fortunate than ourselves and hope that they . . . uh . . . will not always be so unfortunate. Amen.'

The orchestra struck up the first chord of a dirge of Brent's own composition; the school accompanied with something almost resembling the Lord's Prayer. Reverend Rock placed the morning's address on the lectern and began to read.

'We heard not so long ago in the reading how Jesus destroyed the temple and drove out the merchants . . .' He stopped. 'Of course, it wasn't quite the same in the version you heard, but I'm sure that that type of person would have been cast out pretty quickly anyway . . .'

He produced a plug from his pocket and held it up. 'This is a plug.' He looked at it and could not remember what its exact purpose was, suspended before the assembly. 'And . . . and . . .' He had lost his place. The reading had really thrown him. He'd soon punish Simpkin, showing him up like this.

Following the same line of thought that led Reverend Rock to believe that God was working personally for him, before and above everything else, he was now convinced that Simpkin had been the Lee Harvey Oswald of some more intricate plot to assassinate his reputation in front of the whole school.

101

'And . . . Christianity is like electricity: the church is the circuit and Christ the conductor . . . the spirit the electric charge that passes into a body in order to change it. *But . . .* within the church . . .' He leaned forward, warningly, '. . . there are both positive and negative currents. It is your duty, as young Christians, to . . . to . . . know your own voltage.' Well, he wouldn't have to explain it to anyone.

'I'd like to see the Sixth Form after assembly, please,' said Graystone.

The back row affected wide-eyed innocence.

'It was your idea,' said Simon Henley.

'You sent the note,' said Alan Regan.

'I never wanted to do it anyway,' said Stephen Wallis.

The school filed out in rows, accompanied by another orchestral experimentation: this time a mild sabotage of Handel.

Horseplay II: Jockeys

Philip Taylor was sacked from his post as chairman of the newspaper syndicate and it was decided that if the organisation were to regain the stature it once had, a new type of leader should be sought. It was agreed at the pre-election meeting that he (or she – though this was unlikely as the job demanded objectivity and could ill afford the risk of female tears, said the 60% majority of male voters) should be of strong disposition and express a willingness to carry out his duties as he saw fit, even when general opinion went against him. He should have a sharp eye for detecting the machinations of his more malevolent colleagues, particularly those members of the SCR who had enjoyed privileges under the laxity of the old system. Above all, he had to possess specialist knowledge: that of the techniques of being a real pain-in-the-arse.

Symms was the natural choice and, as there were no other contenders, he was elected. His first innovation was to lower the subscription fee from 15p to 10p a week. In addition, an official list of members was drawn up and those on it placed under oath to prevent aliens from obtaining contact with any

102

newspaper. Richard Smith inevitably became the biggest victim under the new regime. The chairman of the syndicate went about his duty fastidiously and as Smith's hand edged its usual way across the table, Symms always appeared from the most unexpected cranny. He would creep up behind the guilty party and snatch the paper in one swift movement:

'Five pence, please, Dick.'

'This is stupid!' Dick would say. His tiny nose and enormously thick lips gave him the appearance of a child's spongy glove-puppet, the nose of which can be pressed wholly into the surface of the face. At Symms' attack, they shrank almost to the point of disappearance as his angry brain sucked them back into his head. 'I bet half the people who read it haven't paid.' Sulking like a child, Smith would slouch away. Every morning the performance was repeated.

Over half term, Smith devised a new plot. He knew that Symms, along with other staff, stayed in the SCR before morning registration to await the day's notices and cover lists. If, therefore, he were to go to the JCR as soon as he arrived at school and read the paper then, he could get through the larger part of it (the headlines, at least) before anyone else arrived. He wondered why he had not thought of it before. After regulating times according to particular days of the week, allowing for fewer notices on the SCR board on Mondays, Smith decided to put his rhythm method into practice.

'Lovely day, isn't it?' Damn. It was Liz Caversham, putting in some early morning preparation.

'Yes, lovely.'

She didn't look up. Good. That was one thing in his favour. Now for the paper. His eyes greedily scanned every available surface in search of *The Guardian*; it was not in its usual place. Ha! There it was. Near the window. Folded and tucked away – hidden? he wondered – down the side of an armchair. Next, movement number two. How could he move from one side of the room to the other, without appearing to act suspiciously? He glanced over each shoulder in turn, took one deep breath and then went for it. His eyes registered *The Guardian*, Monday, and 23p, before a large, hairy hand reached over his right shoulder. He turned quickly and came face to face with several more hirsute features, including two bushy eyebrows from

103

under which two brown eyes glared menacingly. Malcolm Hewitt. Typical of a P.E. teacher to think he could wander around the school aimlessly at any time.

'Sorry, you're not a member of the syndicate,' said Hewitt, snatching the paper from Smith's grasp. 'Unless, of course, you'd like to give me the standard fee . . . No, I'll tell you what I'll do . . . Temporary reader's fee . . . let me see . . . 10p over five days, two dailies, that's a penny a day . . . hm, but that's members' rates. I don't want the union onto me. Tell you what – 5p. Can't be fairer than that. No, better make it six. Don't know how much you've read.'

Smith's eyes bulged with fury. He had loathed Hewitt ever since he discovered that it was he who had put his name onto the National Front mailing list.

'Give me back that bloody paper,' he snarled. His eyes reached forwards out of their sockets, magnifying the red veins in the whites of his eyes.

'6p, please,' Hewitt insisted, waving the paper in front of Smith's nose.

Smith swiped at it and missed. Hewitt lifted it high above his head. His height gave him the final advantage over the other man's short and stocky frame. Smith gave a little jump, and surrendered. His spongy features sprang into action all at once, occasionally settling themselves into a single, two-second purple glare.

'Stop being so damn childish and give me the paper!' he shouted.

'Temper, temper. I think I'm going to have to report you to our members. And they won't like this one little bit' – he waggled his finger – 'not one teeny weeny little bit.' Hewitt walked away, taking the paper with him. The staff room had begun to fill.

'I'll get you for this . . . you just see if I don't.' Smith's bright purple, pointed ears and stubby red nose marched furiously away.

Horseplay III: Mares

Fatness is preferable to ugliness. Belinda Ash, captain of Team

'B', kept this in mind as the range of choice narrowed. They had reached approximately two thirds of the way down the barrel. Now only the dregs were left.

'Elizabeth Ellison,' said Belinda, adding the surname to indicate that these were the less desirable team-mates. A groan spread like a worsening disease down the line of the team. Now that they themselves were safe, they hated the idea of being forced to accept a stranger into their midst. Besides, Elizabeth had a stammer.

There were five girls left. Marjory Lewis would be last. Marjory Lewis was always last. She was fat *and* ugly. She was also a rotten athlete. Susan Jefferson was a swot; Jane Williams was cock-eyed; Annette Stevenson smelt of damp dishcloths; and Linda Mostyn was so fat she was liable to burst before the final whistle blew.

'Katrin, your turn,' said Esther Lamb.

Team 'A' gave encouragement to their leader.

'Choose Jane, she's okay really.'

'Mostyn – no-one'll be able to pass her, she'll block all four lanes.'

'Smelly Stevie, they won't come near her.'

Katrin listened carefully to the advice of her team-mates standing at the front of the line: the ones who were always in demand from both sides and went quickly like cuddly toys in a raffle.

'Hurry up, please, Katrin.'

'I suppose I'll have to have Jane,' sulked Katrin.

Jane's eyes widened with joy. She had never been selected this early on before. This sudden movement, however, made Katrin realise that they would be lucky if Jane could keep her one good eye on the running-track, let alone the relay baton. She changed her mind.

'No, Linda.' Linda *was* fat, but she was quite pretty underneath it all.

There were four left. It was Belinda's turn again. She scanned the group. They shuffled closer together, as if trying to hide each other's disabilities.

'Can't we just carry on with the teams we've already got?' asked Belinda.

'Choose! Or you won't be running at all.'

105

A green, snotty bubble appeared at the entrance to Annette Stevenson's right nostril. It expanded and contracted like an oxygen bag, indicating the quick, nervous rhythm of her breathing. Belinda's stomach turned. Well, at least she was one step further towards making a decision – fatness is preferable to dirtiness.

'Hurry *up*, Belinda!'

'Jefferson,' said Belinda.

'Jefferson who?'

'Swotty Susan.'

Susan did not object to the insult. She rushed thankfully to the rear of Belinda's team. She had recently read a story in a magazine in which a girl who is generally disliked and rejected from the society of other girls, is suddenly discovered to be a great tennis player. She brings glory to the school and thereby popularity to herself. Well, she would do the same . . . The rest of the team will be standing at the side of the track, uninterested in her progress. Then, a gasp from the Games teacher will make them turn their heads in her direction. There she will be. Running towards them with such ease as to make them marvel at her flight. She will win a cup to share with her team. By next summer, she will be the first person selected for Team 'A'; maybe she will be a captain herself.

Now there were three.

The decisions were becoming harder to make. What *is* ugliness, after all? thought Katrin. Beauty is in the eye of the beholder. But there *were* exceptions. Marjory was most definitely ugly, by anyone's standards. Form Five boys said that she had shown them her tits because they didn't believe she was a size 40D. Rodney Morris told Jonathan Ellison that she had bigger tits than his mum, and his mum had fed quads from hers. Dannie Stone said that Richard James said that Kevin Grayle said that his friend had 'had' her and it had put him off meat for life.

Cock-eyes. Well, that was an accident of birth. Fatness and smelliness can be helped; Lewis and Stevenson could do something about that if they wanted to. Katrin felt a sudden surge of compassion towards Jane, particularly as she had already raised her hopes once before that afternoon. But then she knew that Smelly Stevie could run – at least as fast as Greta Lyon – and she had been picked when the barrel was half-full.

'Uh . . . I'll have Jane.' Cock-eyes *did* have the edge over smelliness, it was no good trying to pretend otherwise.

This time Jane did not dare show any glimmer of pleasure. She walked tentatively to the back of Katrin's team.

And then there were two. Belinda, Team 'B', had arrived at her last choice. She observed the flesh folding over the waistband of Marjory's skirt. Her ankles looked swollen and her eyes seemed to have been pressed into two slits by the enormous billowing of her fat cheeks. She delivered a smile in an attempt to bribe the team captain. Her face expanded widthways, as if something were pressing on her head from above. This sudden change of expression proved significant. Belinda noticed, for the first time, that Marjory was wearing a brace. A new, brightly shining pair of teeth-cuffs that glinted as they caught the sun. What if Marjory were to fall and choke on the contraption? Suppose she lost it mid-field? Belinda decided she could not be held responsible for such a liability.

'Stevie, then.' Annette walked along the length of her team, her odour drifting in the breeze, an airy baton passing from one girl's nose to the next.

Marjory Lewis stood alone at the front. Her accusers faced her like a firing-squad. Marjory Lewis. Fat. Ugly. Orthodontically unsound. She watched four girls from each team take up their positions at the relay starting-points. They went down on their haunches and stared ahead, alert creatures waiting to pounce on an unsuspecting victim. Esther Lamb raised the starting gun in the air and held it at arm's length. Slowly, she lowered it in a curve; it travelled 90° and reached a parallel with the head of Marjory Lewis. *READY.* The teacher could see the girl's nose above the barrel. Marjory Lewis. Reject. *STEADY.* The gun's nose found the target of her right temple. Marjory Lewis. *GO!*

CHAPTER SIX

METHODS OF ASSESSMENT

Many common ailments and injuries of horses are the result of basic mismanagement, and it is essential that all animals are regularly checked for physical fitness.

The causes of lameness are various: bad riding and fast work on slow ground are among the most common. Working a horse to the point of excessive tiredness is also likely to cause lameness, if not more serious injuries.

Conditions in the stable also affect the physical well-being of a horse. Bad conditions may cause rheumatism, which in itself can cause lameness; while laminitis, an inflammation caused by a horse's reluctance to move, may be a result of its inability to do so in cramped conditions. Over-feeding may increase inflammation and it is therefore important that a horse with a tendency to greed be watched, when infected. In cases of extreme neglect – continual standing in dirty, wet conditions, bad shoeing etc. – thrush may occur; while in cramped conditions, treads can be made on a horse's hindfeet by the front toe of the horse behind. When riding, horses should be kept a full horse-length apart at all times.

Salmon had sent his apologies and regretted that an urgent matter regarding the redeployment of staff had called him away to a meeting with the County Director of Education. The appointment of a teacher to the Biology Scale 1 post was therefore delegated to Graystone. He was enjoying his new responsibilities and began to regret his decision to retire at the end of the year. For the first time, staff were being forced to acknowledge the importance of a good deputy on a sinking ship. Miss Beak extended his privileges and allowed him an unlimited supply of paper, while Matron used him as the theme for at least one main meal a week. Feeling under obligation to consume double portions as a sign of appreciation, however, meant that Graystone's already weak heart suffered untold damage; any fantasy he entertained regarding a captaincy at long last, would soon be destroyed by a second heart attack. But for the moment he was happy, and Dorothy Crashaw was sent to fetch the first candidate from Brian Cottrill's office.

She returned with Elliot Campbell, first in alphabetical order, and led him to the centre of the room. 'Number One,' she announced to the assembled party.

'Thank you, Mrs Crashaw, that will be all for the moment,' said Graystone.

Elliot Campbell stood facing Graystone, who was seated at his desk; on his left sat the County Advisor for Biology, Frank Spawn; on his right, Riverside's Head of Science, Alan Richards; and behind, Mrs Wiseman, a parent governor.

Into the Ring

> *Elliot Campbell, 18 hands 2″*
> *Alan King, 17 hands 1″*
> *Sarah Kirby, 15 hands 4″*
> *Frank Peters, 18 hands*
> *Lucy Pugh, 15 hands*

'Right, ladies and gentlemen,' said Graystone. 'Elliot Campbell, 18 hands 2″ and the tallest of our candidates. A very fine specimen, I think you'll agree.' Graystone reached out a hand and smoothed Campbell's hair. 'Fine coat – smooth, shiny. A little ruffled round the ears, though.'

Number One self-consciously shook his head.

'How old?' asked Frank Spawn.

'Now, let me see . . . hm . . . just turned thirty. Quite solid for his age, I suppose. Just trot over to Mrs Wiseman, please.'

'Hm,' said Mrs Wiseman, wrenching Campbell's jaws apart. 'Looks a bit long in the tooth to me. Galvayne's Groove not visible.'

'Turn around, please,' said Graystone.

'Quite a nice little mover,' said Richards. 'No signs of lameness. Could you just bend forward a little . . . Sit . . . Stand . . . Raise a hoof . . . Hm . . . Possibly a little stiff.'

'Mr Spawn, if you'd like to take a closer look,' said Graystone.

The County Advisor left his seat and walked over to Number One. 'Just raise a leg again, please.' Campbell did so. Spawn examined the sole. 'Ha! Canker, if I'm not mistaken. Let's see another. Hm. Windgalls . . . Curb . . . Hock . . .' He moved his way up Campbell's leg. 'Pretty good, on the whole. Slight tenderness around the hock – thoroughpin, I'd say, but nothing that a bit of massage won't disperse. Good for a few more years yet, I'd say. Firm genitals, too,' he added, squelching Campbell between the legs.

'Right, that'll be all for now,' said Graystone. 'You may sit down.'

'Where do you come from?'

'Oxford,' said Lucy Pugh.

'Did you travel down today?'

'No.'

'Yesterday?'

'I'm staying with friends.'

'Oh,' Sarah Kirby now turned to the candidate seated on her left. 'What's your name?'

'Frank Peters.'

'Have you taught before?'

'Yes. I was teaching at a school in Suffolk for just over five years.'

Sarah's heart sank. It was bad enough when the other candidates said they had been teaching one year, let alone five.

'I left teaching to go back to university,' he continued. 'I've just finished my PhD.'

'Oh.'

She won't get it, thought Lucy Pugh. Far too agitated. Never let the other candidates unnerve you, that's the secret. This was her tenth interview of the month, so she should know.

The door opened. The candidates watched. A tray edged

itself around the door, followed by Mrs Crashaw. Frank Peters rose to help the secretary manoeuvre herself in.

Why didn't I think of that, thought Alan King. 'It's a lovely school,' he said quickly.

'Shall I be mother?' giggled Sarah. She poured from one of the large jugs of coffee into four cups. 'One lump or two?' she asked Frank Peters.

'Don't risk all that,' said Graystone to Richards. 'Not until you've seen the other candidates. Remember the Derby.' Richards redeposited £2 in his wallet. 'Right,' announced Graystone, 'that puts Number One at 20–1 to win. Quite a good chance of your being the favourite on those sort of odds, Mr Campbell.'

The door reopened. Campbell appeared, pawing the ground before emerging fully into the room. He gave a broad smile, and frothy saliva spread like a horse's bit across his front teeth.

'How did it go?' asked Sarah.

'Not bad, I think.'

'What did they ask you?'

'All the usual things. How would I teach this, that, or the other. What would I do if this, this and this happened.' Campbell avoided specifics. After all, he had received no hints prior to the ordeal. He could not resist telling of his pièce de résistance, however. 'Oh yes, what approach would I take when teaching the reproduction organs of a mammal.'

'What did you say?'

'Well, I told them that it all depended upon what approach one took to education. If, for example, one advocated Piaget's . . .'

'Mr King next, please,' said Mrs Crashaw, popping her head around the door.

'Good luck,' said Sarah.

'Good luck,' said Campbell.

'Number Two: Mr King, ladies and gentlemen,' said Graystone.

Mrs Wiseman frowned. The last time she had placed a bet on a 'King', she had lost £10.

111

'Would you come just a little closer, please,' asked Graystone. 'I think you've got a slight inflammation around the heels.' King shifted his weight and the skin around his heels cracked; a greasy discharge rolled down onto the carpet. 'Cracked heels,' stated Graystone, knowledgeably. 'Clear up in no time. Make sure your heels are always dried properly,' he warned, shaking a remonstrative finger. 'Back to the middle, please.'

'Right, ladies and gentlemen. Alan King, 17 hands 1". Pretty full track record. Five schools in two years. Let's hear you neigh, Mr King.' Number Two gave a high-pitched roar. 'Hm, a bit hoarse,' said Graystone. 'Could be the sign of a chill. I bet you're one of those horses who throws his rug off, eh?' King neighed again.

'Nice rounded haunches,' said Mrs Wiseman, her earlier distress placated by the splendid physique before her.

'Testicles need a good harness,' said Spawn, grovelling between the legs. 'Hello, hello, a bit damp too. Bad, that. Sign of an angry temperament.'

'Where on earth did you read that?' asked Richards.

'It just is, that's all.'

'That's ridiculous.'

'Gentlemen, gentlemen,' said Graystone. 'This is no time to dispute it. We are all experts in our own field.'

'Such lovely haunches,' said Mrs Wiseman, dribbling.

'Turn around, please,' said Richards. 'Hm. Not bad, I suppose. Not really Grand National material though, on the whole.'

'Stick a rosette in these and they'd shrink to nothing,' said Spawn, struggling with a lost ball.

'Alan, anything more you'd like to say?'

'Well, only about the goggles. I mean, he's just asking to be made a laughing stock of the whole school if he goes round wearing those.'

'Very well,' said Graystone. '50–1, agreed?'

'Agreed.'

'Well?' said Elliot Campbell. Now that his own interview was over, he could relax quite happily in the failures of others when they returned to the enclosure.

'Not very good,' said King. He removed his glasses, the thick lenses of which appeared to press right up against each eyeball, and rubbed his eyes.

He's lying, thought Lucy. That was an old technique.

'Oh, what a shame,' said Campbell, biting his tongue.

'Who's next, then?'

'I think it's me,' said Sarah.

Well, they certainly won't appoint a girl to a Science post, thought Campbell.

'Quite a nice little filly, I think we're all agreed on that, gentlemen, wouldn't you say?'

'Too flabby around the stomach,' said Mrs Wiseman, 'and her hair's too long.'

'Good solid breastbone,' said Spawn.

'Probably good for a quick ride,' said Richards.

'But what's she like over long distance, eh?' said Spawn. pinching one of Number Three's haunches. 'Let's have a look at the other one alongside her. Much easier to compare that way. Mrs Crashaw,' he called, 'bring in Number Four.'

Lucy Pugh hung her head as she was placed beside Sarah Kirby. Once on her feet, her height ensured the loss of all previous confidence.

'Only fifteen hands,' said Richards. 'Would tire easily. I wouldn't put more than a quid each way on this one. The other, 15–1 to win.'

'I'd say 100–1,' said Mrs Wiseman. 'I think we ought to choose an ugly one. You're far too impressionable.'

'I'm sorry, but you're outvoted,' said Graystone. '15–1 on the long-haired filly, agreed? Good. Number Four, I think you might as well return to your stable now. No point in staying until the end of the race when you've fallen at the first fence now, is there? Jolly good. Trot along then. Number Three, do sit down.'

'Phew! I'm glad that's over,' said Sarah.

'Did they ask you any awkward questions?'

'Not really. I diverted their attention with a book I've put together on teaching practice: Form One drawings of plants, and nature poems.'

113

'No one told me I could bring in visual aids,' said Campbell. Damn. They'd really go for that sort of thing.

'No one told me, either,' said Peters.

'But that's not fair,' said King. 'I could have shown them my amoeba in a jam-jar. Or my test-tube chestnut.'

'Mr Peters, please,' said Mrs Crashaw.

'When I say "Go",' said Frank Peters, Number Five, 'I want you to run towards me. Are you ready . . . ? On your marks . . . get set . . . GO!'

And it's Graystone off to a very fine start on the outside three lengths from Spawn but Richards coming up fast on the inside and a long way behind is Wiseman and Graystone beginning to trail now and overtaken by Spawn and it's a close thing between Spawn and Richards with Wiseman still trailing by four lengths and it's Spawn and Richards all the way Spawn and Richards and this is such a close race but at the line it's Spawn first followed by Richards then Wiseman from Graystone in fourth place.

'Good boy, good boy,' said Peters, patting Spawn on the side of his neck. 'Excellent race.' He took four lumps of sugar from the bowl on Graystone's desk and held them out in the palm of his hand. Spawn gobbled furiously. Richards then received three lumps, Mrs Wiseman two, and Graystone puffing, panting and sweating, one.

'How did it go?' asked Alan King.

'Had them eating out of my hand,' said Frank Peters.

Campbell, King and Sarah Kirby tried not to look too discouraged.

'More coffee, anyone?' asked Mrs Crashaw. 'They're likely to take some time deciding.'

He knows he's got it, thinks Campbell, glaring at King. They always do. Like those girls in the beauty contests who then try to look surprised when they're announced as having won.

I bet he's got it, thinks Sarah. He's bound to with a name like Elliot. He's been so confident, right from the start. Probably has a father who plays golf with the Director of Education.

What's the betting they'll give it to the girl, thinks King. Just because she's a girl.

114

I'm sure I've got it, thinks Peters. I was in there the longest and that's always a good sign. And I've played tennis with the governor's husband.

The door opened slowly. The frame became filled with Graystone. Sarah Kirby picked at the skin around her nails; Alan King slouched, affecting nonchalance; Elliot Campbell stared out of the window; Frank Peters sat up straight and looked Graystone in the eye.

'Mr Peters, please . . . Would you come with me?'

Peters stood up slowly. Sarah muttered a 'Well done', King blushed and Campbell frowned. Peters covered his mouth with the palm of his hand: it really was so very difficult not to smirk.

'Of course, you know he's got the same Christian name as the Advisor, do you?' said Campbell, spitefully, when the door had been closed.

'I didn't like the school anyway,' said King.

The Races: Horses for Courses

More horses then ever before are now being put into training for the racing circuit. But without long-term investment geared towards improving both standards and overall quality, the future well-being and prosperity of the racing world is put at risk.

Due to financial pressure, the horses of today are required to begin their racing life much earlier than those of years ago. They are forced into early maturity, whereby size and speed are often developed at the expense of stamina. However, no horse should, in theory, be put forward for racing without its being ready.

EXAMINATION TIMETABLE MAY/JUNE 1984

'O' and 'A' Levels: Sports Hall
Forms 1–4 S,T,A,B,L,E: Normal Classrooms and Lessons
Lower Sixth: Library, Normal Lessons

'Sir . . .'
'Ssh . . .'

'What is it?' whispered Jonathan Hayward, coming to the aid of a distraught Fifth Form boy.

'Sir, we haven't done this play.'

'What do you mean?'

'We did *Billy Liar*. There aren't any questions on it.'

Hayward took the 'O' Level Literature paper and examined it for evidence of Billy Liar. He was nowhere to be found.

'Who's your teacher?' he asked the boy.

'Mr McGill, Sir.'

'Right,' announced Hayward. 'Hands up all those from Mr McGill's Set Two English class who did *Billy Liar* as their set play.' Over thirty hands went up. Hayward tried to stay calm. 'Well, as you may have noticed, there aren't any questions on it. Now don't panic. The . . . er . . . examining board must have made a mistake. I'm sure there's a simple explanation. I'll just go and sort it out. You just carry on with the rest of the paper.'

'Aw, Sir,' said another boy. 'I did the play question first. I wrote on *Saint Joan*.'

'You haven't done *Saint Joan*.'

'The question looked easy, though. And we've done her in History.'

'Look. Settle down, please. Don't attempt the play section until I get back . . . We'll allow them extra time,' he whispered to Alan Richards, on his way out.

Howard returned half an hour later with a set of questions the examining board had agreed to set, in view of McGill's blunder. Fortunately, McGill was supervising another exam that morning, which saved him from the worst of his head of department's wrath.

'It's a mistake anyone could make,' he said, when finally confronted. 'Anyway, I don't like *Saint Joan*.'

Jeanette Hale struggled out of the stock-room where the C.S.E. English Orals were taking place: a telescope, complete with tripod under one arm, three books on astronomy and a signed photograph of Patrick Moore under the other. Patricia White agreed with her head of department that it was by far the most competent talk yet: thoroughly prepared, interesting and

116

delivered in a clear, lively manner. They awarded her eighteen out of twenty.

'Ah, Gary, come in. Take a seat, please.' The next candidate, a lanky boy with black hair, shuffled to the empty chair. Jonathan Hayward handed him a copy of *The Other Side of the Mountain*. 'Will you start reading from the paragraph commencing "At that time there were no sheep . . .", on page 139, please.'

Gary Cooper sniffed. He stared down blankly at the page, wearing an expression that might be interpreted as (a) What do you mean by 'commence'? (b) What's a paragraph? or (c) What-do-I-want-with-C.S.E.s-anyway-when-there-are-three-million-unemployed-and-I-hate-school-too.

Hayward coughed. 'When you're ready, Gary.'

Sniff. ' "At vhat time vhere wuz . . . vhere were no sheep . . . ter . . . ter disturb me . . . us . . . on vhe . . . 'illside." ' Sniff. ' "Ev'ry day me dad 'n' me wen' out lookin' fer somethin' ter eat an' . . . an' nuffin'. . ." '

'Try to read *exactly* what's on the page, Gary,' said Hayward.

Cooper was the tenth candidate of the morning and Hayward's patience had started to wane. Patricia White, his shift co-worker sat, for the most part, motionless and speechless. All right, the Orals were boring, but they had to be done. The kids were nervous enough as it was, without having to be faced with some dummy on the other side of the desk.

'Thank you, Gary. That was fine.' Three out of ten. He was making it up as he went along.

'Why do you think Ralph and his father found the conditions difficult to work in on the hillside?' asked Hayward. Silence. Sniff. 'Do you think it might have had something to do with the contrast with their previous existence?' Silence again. Hayward saw Patricia twitch. She was alive at any rate. 'I mean, they had not lived under such primitive conditions before, had they?'

'No, Sir.'

Hayward smiled in encouragement. At last. Probing was one thing, digging another; but the boy was having to be positively mined. Perhaps a more basic question . . .

'Do you remember the name of their dog?'

Silence, followed by a frown. Cooper's throat twitched. Had they struck gold?

'. . . ? . . . Rover?'

Not even coal. 'No, Gary.' Patricia mouthed a word; not, felt Hayward, in an attempt to help the boy, but to show that she knew the answer. Well so she damn well ought to. She'd heard it ten sodding times in one morning. 'Let's try another. Do you remember the name of the boy?'

'Umm . . .' He was really straining this time. 'Uh . . . No, Sir.'

'You've just been reading about him, Gary.'

'Uh . . .' Eyes creased. 'Don't know, Sir.'

'Have you actually read this book, Gary?'

'Course, Sir.' The boy's eyes opened to a wide, indignant expression: Do you really think, Sir, that after two years of studying English, I would be so foolish as not to read one of the set books . . .?

'Gary – can you say, in all honesty, that you have read this book?'

'No, Sir.'

Always rephrase the question – guaranteed to catch them out. 'Well, we'd better leave the questions, as you clearly won't be able to discuss the book at any great length.'

'I've seen the film, though.'

'Have you, Gary. I'd like to move on and hear your talk now . . . When you're ready, Gary.'

'Uh . . . I collect coins.'

Hayward waited a few seconds before leaning forward in the hope of at least spiritually catching the essence of the three word talk. 'Uh . . . Go on.' There *was* more, surely.

'Well, that's it.'

'Have you many?' asked Patricia.

The sudden intrusion of a new voice made the boy jump. 'Yeah.'

'How long have you been collecting?'

'Ages.'

'Have you any favourites?'

'No.'

You must have some fucking favourites. Everyone has at

least one sodding favourite, thought Hayward. 'Have you brought any with you?'

'No.'

'What do you call someone who collects coins?' asked Patricia.

'. . . Coin-collector?'

'Right, Gary. Thanks very much. We'll leave it there for today.' Hayward managed a Don't-look-so-nervous-you-did-all-right-really smile. What a moron, he thought.

Cooper quickly left his seat. At the door, he hesitated and turned round. 'That's not my real hobby, though.'

'I said you can go now, Gary,' Hayward insisted.

'I'm more interested in corpses. Have you ever seen a dead body? My aunt had one throw up all over her. See, she was a nurse and after they'd tied up the jaws of this old man, they rolled him over and out it came. All the muscles loosen up, see. They're quiet, corpses. Like the late bus home when the last person's got off . . . I'm going to be an undertaker,' he smiled, and left the room.

Silence.

'One for the talk, do you agree?' said Hayward. His final shred of sympathy had just been eaten up.

'I didn't think he was that bad,' said Patricia.

'One of yours, is he?'

'Yes, he is, actually.'

It was easy to spot which pupils belonged to which teachers. The pupils kept their eyes fixed on the eyes of their own, striking up a bond, a curiously private conspiracy against the other teacher present. It was just hard luck on those whose teacher was not working their shift.

'Yes . . . come in, Stephen.' Stephen Rendell took his seat. 'You can start when you're ready.' For convenience sake, Hayward chose the same passage. 'The paragraph commencing "At that time there were no sheep . . ." on page 139.'

I hate this book, thought Hayward. I hate this supercilious, know-it-all little dick Ralph, who haunts every damn school reader. Why are our educational institutions plagued by Ralphs? Kids with monster penknives who can draw fire from wood, sharpen blades on stones, hunt wild boar and roast them on a spit. Hardened little brats were these Ralphs: took to the

119

hills at the age of three with only a knapsack strung to their backs; happened to find a sick old man to tend in a cave. And why did they always have archaeologist uncles? I hate Ralph, his father *and* his dog on the other side of the mountain. Hayward bit his bottom lip.

Stephen Rendell had finished reading. Hayward asked the statutory questions; the boy answered.

'Did you enjoy this book, Stephen?'

'Uh, yes, Sir.'

'*Really?*'

'No, Sir. I thought it was boring.'

'Fine. Now can we have your talk, please.'

'I collect fish.' This time there was definitely more coming. 'Well I *did*, anyway. But they're all dead. The first ones I bought died, so I poured the water out and changed the plants and gravel and bought some more. Then, after a week, they died too. So I poured out that water and changed those plants, put some more gravel in and bought some more fish. Well, they died too!' The boy's face was strawberry with embarrassment and vanilla with fear. Hayward softened. '. . . and they died too,' he heard for the enth time.

He hardened again. 'And what was causing their death?'

The boy's face stopped mid-horror. His mouth opened and closed like a gill; no sound came from it. Rendell had not expected so early an interruption. Now his mind reeled fast forward to the end of the story. 'So now I collect coins.'

Next came three talks in which Hayward managed to sound at least half-interested: My family, Tennis, and The Peace Movement, the latter by Carol Lewis who, during the previous term, had been suspended for beating up Rebecca Easton. Hayward had, however, completely failed to sustain interest in the penultimate talk before lunch: the rules governing the relegation of football clubs out of the fourth division..

The final candidate of the morning wheeled in a long box, standing upright, about the size of a coffin. Three gold stars and a moon decorated each side. From behind it stepped Susan Kingsley, a girl from Hayward's class.

'Uh . . . Susan . . . do sit down. Is this er . . .?'

'For my talk. You said we could bring things in.'

'Of course. Yes, of course.'

Susan read. Hayward gave her nine out of ten for both the reading and the questions. He was really very hungry by now, his bladder was full and he found that generosity helped spur the morning on.

'Right. If you'd like to give us your talk,' he said, indicating the box.

Susan remained seated and produced a photograph album. 'My parents have always had a lot to do with the entertainment world, so from when I was about five I used to help them out, get things ready for their shows and things like that.' Pictures of John Kingsley ('The King') in exposing, black silk trousers; Tina Kingsley ('Hot Cat') in . . . or rather out, of a more exposing tiger-skin dress. 'And this is me.'

'Lovely.'

'Pretty.' Even Patricia looked interested.

Susan worked her way through the album. She directed her comments more towards Hayward, as if trying to draw him into a secret: two children in league against an adult bystander.

She closed the album. 'And now,' she said, 'I want to show you a trick my father taught me.' She stood up and went over to the box. 'This,' she said, 'is a magic coffin.' She opened the door. Inside, it was painted completely black. 'Now, I'd like one volunteer, please.'

'I don't think we really have time, Susan,' said Hayward.

'One volunteer,' said the girl, firmly. She stood like a sentry at the side of the box, her eyes fixed firmly ahead.

'Go on, Mr Hayward,' laughed Patricia.

'I think you, Miss White.'

'Oh no, really. I don't like the dark.'

'You won't notice it once you're inside.'

'I really don't . . .'

'Go *on*,' said Hayward.

'Well, if you promise to let me out if I call.'

'Of course,' Susan smiled.

Patricia went across to the other side of the desk. 'What exactly are you going to do? I mean, what *is* it?'

'I told you. It's a magic coffin. Step inside.' Susan held the door open while the teacher settled herself. 'All right?'

'Mm.' Patricia's voice shook slightly. She pressed her palms against the insides of the box, as if preparing for sudden movement.

'I'm going to shut the door now,' said Susan.

'Don't forget – if I call, let me out at once.'

'Of course.' Susan closed the door firmly shut and locked it with a key she took from a string around her neck. 'It's soundproof,' she smiled sardonically at Hayward.

'Now, I've learnt two tricks, but I think I'll just show you the one. It's an old one but still very popular.'

Susan placed a small attaché-like case on the desk and opened it. A row of glittering silver knives, each about a foot long, were lined up neatly, bright and shining as a new box of school crayons. She ran a finger along them; her nail brought a dull, muffled keyboard note from each. She looked up from her broken reflection and smiled again at Hayward: a smile that seemed to take minutes to unfold.

'You . . . uh . . .?' he said.

'There are twelve holes.' said Susan, with authority. 'I'll take six and you can take six.'

Hayward looked from the knives to the magic coffin. 'B. . . But that box is barely more than a foot wide.' He tested a blade to see if it sank into its handle upon application of pressure. it was solid. 'Look . . . I . . .'

'You're not scared, are you?' The girl turned her head to one side. Part of her upper lip twisted into a slightly sneering smile.

'Of course not.'

'Here, take these.' She handed Hayward six knives and came out from behind the desk. 'I'll go first.'

Susan took a knife and ran a finger along the blade. It nipped the top and a drop of blood trickled like an inkspot down the smooth metal. She felt along the front of the magic coffin, as if feeling for a vein from which to take a blood sample. She put the tip of the blade against a hole that would be level with the teacher's heart. Hayward's mouth dried. He listened for any sound that might give some indication of the progress of events inside. Slowly, the girl pushed the knife into the hole. Hayward strained forward. It was most definitely going in. Did the box just rock slightly?

'Your turn.' Susan wiped the moisture that had formed at the corners of her mouth. Hayward stepped forward. She squeezed him at the elbow. 'Which part do you want to take?' She pressed his arm down to his side before leading his hand forward, against its will, to the box. Sweat tickled his forehead. 'Here, take this one.' Susan placed the tip of the knife against a hole that would correspond with the teachers crotch. Hayward stretched his lips and felt them crack with dryness. 'Now push it in,' whispered the girl. 'Go on, it won't bite.'

Hayward's hand was visibly shaking. With his other hand he wiped his forehead. 'I . . . I can't,' he said.

'I'll help you.' His accomplice took his fist into her own cold palm. She managed to push it to within two inches of the box, then it put up resistance. 'Go on, you can't stop now. Put it right in.' She was now clutching his fist tightly and he felt her nails digging into him. The sharp pain caused his fist to relax and now she was gaining control over his movements. She had pushed the knife in completely and was pulling back and forth, in and out. 'Harder, harder,' she said, and now she was in total control of his hand. In Out In Out Harder Harder Harder. Hayward felt his hand slipping in the sweat from each palm, and the knife handle burning his flesh. The rhythm of their joined fists pummelled with a hollow knock each time the handle came up against the wood. In Out In Out Faster Faster Faster. Hayward's whole body reeled away from the box as the slippery knife fell from his grasp on its withdrawal. The girl's cheeks were red. She was smiling. Hayward bent over his desk, his back to her. He heard a key turn in a lock; a laugh scuttled across the air.

'Well, come on, tell me. What did you *do* to me? I'm all ears. Was I supposed to disappear or something?'

Hayward turned round. Susan was wheeling the magic coffin away. At the door, she stopped. 'Oh, did you want to ask me any questions?'

Patricia looked at Hayward. 'Uh, no, no, I don't think so,' he said. 'That'll be all.'

He avoided direct confrontation with the girl and fixed his eyes instead upon the three gold stars and silver moon on the door of the box. Somehow, though, he knew without looking the expression on her face. For years to come, he would remember each night her tilting smile; the reflection of a row of knives slicing her eyes; and a voice beating the rhythm of his fist Harder Harder Harder.

CHAPTER SEVEN

QUALITIES OF LEADERSHIP

Half a league, half a league,
Half a league onward. . .
Into the valley of Death
Rode the six hundred.

Alfred, Lord Tennyson

HORSE OPERA: Affectionately derogatory term for the
WESTERN, probably occasioned equally by the fact that the hero's
best friend was usually his horse, and by the rise of the singing
cowboy after the advent of the all-talking movie had led to a decline
in the all-action western.

The Fontana Dictionary of Modern Thought

They Shoot Horses, Don't They?

RIVERSIDE COMPREHENSIVE SCHOOL
D-DAY MEMORIAL SERVICE
WEDNESDAY 6TH JUNE 1984

Programme

Rossini's William Tell Overture	The School Orchestra
	Conductor: Mr M. Brent
Hymn: O God Our Help in Ages Past	All
Reading: I Corinthians ch. 13:1–13	The Deputy-Head
Prayer and Lord's Prayer	The Reverend Mr Rock
Hymn: Sound the Battle Cry	All
Poems: Anthem for Doomed Youth	The Head Girl
by Wilfred Owen	

124

The Soldier	The Head Boy
by Rupert Brooke	
The Names of the Fallen	The Headmaster
Address	Major D. M. Barton
Hymn: Onward Christian Soldiers	All

'Walk! Put your blazer on!' shouted Miss Calne.

The last pupils made their late scrabbled entry into the school hall. Others, inside, bored by the delay, started to unravel from the lines their form teachers had gone to such lengths to create.

'Linton! Shut up, unless you want a taste of detention,' shouted Malcolm Hewitt. Linton, standing in the middle of 4T's row of boys, raised innocent, staring eyes.

'Miss, Susan feels sick,' said Andrea Summers of 1S, to Julia Soames, the form teacher. Susan's green face whitened, blushed, and then with a marbled effect of all three colours, fell to the floor.

'Something funny, lad?' Geoff Symms picked on a boy seated with the first years at the front. 'I said, is there something amusing you, lad?' The boy continued to stare at the ceiling, his head tilted back and a distorted grin spreading across his face.

'Sir, I think he's having a fit. He's an epileptic.'

Disruptive influences removed, the atmosphere settled and the form teachers patrolled their respective rows once more, carrying out a final inspection. They checked again for combed hair, clean faces, hands and finger-nails; and no ear-rings, chains, or jewellery of any other sort. People in a passing plane might have mistaken the sight for that of a moderately well turned out battalion. When the teachers were satisfied that their own form was in with a good chance of winning Graystone's 'smartest class' medal, they retired to the end of their rows and stood sentry, awaiting the visitors.

Remembrance Day, back in November, had been rather a shoddy affair. Owing to the arrangement of examination desks in the Sports hall and decorators' equipment in the main hall, the school had been unable to gather as one body. The day had therefore been commemorated by each individual class at services held in form rooms; in the knowledge that a big forty-year anniversary of D-Day was not far away, it was assumed adequate. A sort of mini-baptism. It was not foreseen at the time that Form Five and the Upper Sixth would be absent for reasons of external examinations; neither would it have been known that one of the Old Soldier guests, booked for November would, in the meantime, die. Despite diminished numbers, however, it was his substitute who now led the rest of the invited party from the back of the hall towards the stage.

Muffled snorts, like those from discontented horses, came from the middle of rows. The Old Fogies, for some never-quite-explained reason, were always a source of great mirth, particularly the ones who had to be manoeuvred onto the stage by staff. It was embarrassed, as opposed to mocking laughter: the kind that can inexplicably well up from the pit of the stomach when you are informed of an unhappy event; escapist laughter that is the easiest retreat from being forced to acknowledge the seriousness of events past. And also, it disguised the future: mocked time, dared it to make youth grow old, yet all the while hoping that Old Foginess would leave them well alone. But now, in 1984, there was something akin to hysteria mixed in with that laughter. The Upper School appeared to be undergoing greater delirium in the back than ever before; even First Formers, normally wide-eyed, innocent and serious on such awesome occasions, managed a few smirks. This was a new breed of laughter, tinged with fear. Its greater hysteria was a form of panic, a sudden realization that the disguise had been ripped away: Old Foginess might *not* come to them all, and now they hoped and prayed for it with all their hearts. In some obscure way they envied these old men: they had fought and made war, yet theirs was a war which had allowed the continuance of Nature's course; given them the time that, for many of their colleagues, had been snatched away; years that, should a war strike the younger generation, would not be worth living. And so there was also resentment in their laughter: resentment that these Old Fogies who had created the future, would by mere accident escape it.

Today the staff's attentions were riveted on Kenneth Salmon. The memorial service would be his first public appearance since the Fifth Form Parents' Evening and, as he entered the hall, halfway along the line between guests and senior staff, an air of suspense spread along the rows of pupils as

126

he approached. Their bodies stiffened instinctively and stretched upwards; when he had passed, they relaxed once more, falling softly in waves unable to summon up sufficient energy to break. Today, the Headmaster seemed to possess the power of walking through them, combing them with his presence. They rose and held a brief moment of static power, before falling once more to settle as one.

Salmon's cloistered life had done little to alter his physical appearance. His hair looked no greyer than it had before and, apart from his slightly sunken cheeks, his face had retained its rather indistinct smoothness of feature. Only now his forehead was set in a permanent frown, which creased the skin around his eyes and intensified his stare. As he walked towards the stage he seemed to notice nothing around him; he moved with the resignation of a predestined man. Suddenly he stopped. The senior staff, following behind, halted awkwardly and trafficked into each other: Graystone took the weight of Miss Calne; Alex Stuart, John Lewis and Brian Cottrill jerked and locked crotch to buttocks; and Reverend Rock, at the rear, rolled into them, solid as the stone which sealed Jesus' tomb.

Salmon, oblivious to the commotion behind and the Old Fogies struggling with the stage ahead, crouched down. He peered intently at the floor surrounding him, as if searching for a lost contact lens. Using both hands, he mimed an action similar to that of the school nurse when pawing for nits in pupils' hair. Then he sighed, stood up and moved on. The clenched stillness released itself and the noise rose.

'*Quiet!*' yelled Graystone, from the front of the stage. 'You may sit, Form One.' Form One, presumably because their bodies were less energetic, were allowed the privilege of seats on Special Occasions, and they sat noisily. '*Stand!*' More noise. 'Let's try it again, Form One . . . Sit.' With each rise and fall, the noise increased. Graystone's orders then rose another note, and both sides, like alternate hands, continued to slap one on top of the other. Form One, in the knowledge that their milky year was coming to a close, were preparing for the future.

'Oh, don't go on, Harold. Leave them be. Anyone would think they were children.' Salmon pushed his deputy aside. Graystone nodded in obedience and swallowed an enormous lump in his throat. He blinked several times in the hope of flicking back the red he felt rising in his cheeks and the hurt pressing behind his eyes. Jonathan Hayward, standing at the back of the hall with 6L, blushed for him. He felt as if he wanted to snatch Graystone from the stage, like a parent unable to bear the humiliation of his child. Feeling a compulsion to move, he side-stepped his way to Geoff Symms. Neither man spoke, but each felt less isolated.

Graystone clasped his hands behind his back and tugged nervously at the jacket of his black suit. This was the suit he had been going to keep for funerals alone, but after the sudden recovery of the uncle in whose honour it had been purchased, it had been hanging stagnant in the wardrobe. He therefore lengthened his list of Suitable Occasions, and D-Day, particularly the fortieth anniversary, had seemed an appropriate one. But now, on the stage, he felt vastly overdressed. Salmon was looking shabby and worn: fading brown trousers, a grey shirt, black jacket, no tie and a graduation gown covered in patches of blue and pink chalk-dust. Graystone thought he looked just like a pantomime horse and cast himself as the villain of the piece. He felt that, given the choice, the audience would boo him offstage and shout More More from this Barabbas. He felt both sorry and slightly resentful at this realisation: sorry for the man, the Salmon he wanted to remember, lost in his costume; and resentful of the fact that, unknown to the audience, he had been riding this creature, incapable of making the slightest judgment or decision itself, for the past school year. They fell for the outward impression, the show; while he, calling out Walk, Trot, Gallop, Sit, Stand, was regarded as the evil one. But his resentment went back further than today, this moment. He realized it had been inching its way through him over many years. Last year – what was it then? That new teacher who hadn't pulled his weight? That rude child? And the year before? And the year before that? Resentment that stemmed from his inability to confront the things that threatened the existence of the old order and therefore his status within it; an order that dedicated itself to the moral, spiritual and physical welfare of the young people within it. All those years behind the scenes – for what? To stand by and watch them go unnoticed? Who was it they patted on the back? Not he, the rider, the villain with a whip in his hand; instead, this bumbling, patch-coated, senseless pantomime horse. 'Don't go on, Harold.' No, don't go on. He was glad he was not going on. Let him be a villain in peace. Graystone smiled. He rather liked his new role as Enemy of the People.

'Let us begin our service . . .' Salmon's voice was almost a whisper. Major Barton craned his neck and Reverend Rock hooked his good ear in the palm of his hand.

Graystone leaned forward. 'I don't think they can hear you at the back, Headmaster,' he said, tactfully.

'What . . .?' Salmon looked quizzical, tossed his head around and bellowed, as if delivering orders mid-battle. '*Can-you-hear-me-at-the-back?*' The Addressed were too embarrassed to answer, as if the head's voice had stripped the air to a rawness too tender to touch. 'I said, Can you hear me at the back?' His voice resumed its normal pitch, and several 'Yessirs' came in response. 'Then let us commence our service with the hymn "O God Our Help in Ages Past".' Marcus Brent managed to raise his baton and start the orchestra just in time to drown Salmon's afterthought. 'A little ironic, I think, under the circumstances.'

During the hymn, Salmon made a close inspection of his gown, as if searching for a secret passage through which he might be able to escape. What was he doing up here, dressed in this silly costume? Then he faced the pupils. And what were all those things down below, all dressed exactly the same? No room for individuality. They'd just as soon shoot one as any other. Didn't they realise how silly they looked? If all their heads were shaved, how much hair would there be? How many garments of clothing would it go to make? Why were they standing in those lines? Why didn't they run away? Who can force them to stand in rows? Why do they listen to orders? How very, very silly they were. Salmon smiled.

The hymn ended. A French horn farted in the sudden silence. The Head sat and Graystone took his place at the lectern.

'The reading this morning is taken from the First Book of Corinthians, chapter 13, verses 1–13.'

Look at him, thought Salmon. He loves it. A fat black capsule. Look at all of them. They make the pupils their junkies. Teachers are more addictive than glue. They make themselves so. Make the pupils believe that without each one of them, the body would die. They even believe it themselves. Spend their time trying to convince each other of the importance of their own individual existence. So they ram themselves down the throat of the pupils, the school, each other. They have to say, Look, you're taking me; you realize that without me, you'd have been dead a long time ago. And they stick in the throat. They are all residents of the same bottle. I have swallowed them all, one by one. Now I will put a finger to the back of my throat and vomit them away.

'And now abideth . . .' The finale to Graystone's reading was disturbed by violent coughing behind as Salmon choked on his right forefinger. '. . . *faith, hope and charity* . . .' shouted Graystone. Major Barton thrashed Salmon on the back, resulting in greater nasal and guttural frenzy. '. . . but the greatest of these . . .' said Graystone, desperately trying to contain his anger, '. . . is charity.' He slapped the sides of the Bible together.

Salmon's whole body heaved forward in a paroxysm of retching. Now I have them, he thought. I have put my finger to the back of my throat and scooped them out. I have brought them up through my body, and outside the body they cannot survive. It gives me pleasure to feel their breathlessness; their suffocating inside my mouth. In a moment, I will spit them out. They have lost their souls in my body. Now, they are nothing. I spit them into my white handkerchief and crush them in my hand. I feel the last of their life, soft, in the clench of my fingers. I will prove that the body can survive while they remain outside it. I will show them I am still alive without them.

Following the prayer, the school joined in the Revised Version of Brent's composition of the Lord's Prayer. 'Sorry about this,' whispered Salmon to Major Barton. When the Head Girl delivered 'Anthem for Doomed Youth' after the next hymn, he whispered again: 'Bet you didn't see much of that in the trenches;' and during the Head Boy's rendering of 'The Soldier': 'Send them all to the army, that's what I say.'

The school remained standing for the Headmaster's reading of the Names of the Fallen. Eyes were fixed permanently on Salmon, as though by their very stare they might hold his composure together.

'Today,' he started, 'is a most solemn occasion.' A thousand foreheads squelched up seriously. 'We are here to commemorate the fortieth anniversary of D-Day. I will read the names of the brave men who gave their lives during the Second World War.' There was a sigh of relief. Now it was just a matter of form.

Salmon coughed and took the list from the lectern. He glanced once more at the audience, so serious, so perfect in their rows, and wanted to laugh. They just looked so silly.

'S. Amber, J. P. Armitage, L. J. Broadstreet, P. S. T. Bynon, T. K. Byron, R. Campbell, S. A. Crawford, L. M. Davies, P. Davies, N. H. Davison.' What a bore this was. If they wanted the list of names, all they had to do was go to the back of the hall and read the commemoration plaques. Salmon removed a pen from the inside of his jacket and continued.

'B. T. Edwards . . .?' He paused and looked around the hall. 'Absent. N. S. Fergusson . . .? . . . Absent.' He continued down the list, marking a large 'O' against each of the names. When he came to the name 'S. Noodel', he started to giggle. He pulled his lips together and called out the name especially loud, in the hope that this might intensify its seriousness.

'*S. Noodel!*'

The silence that followed Noodel's journey through the air was too tempting to leave empty and Salmon filled it with a laugh which, in trying to disguise it, came more as a nasal spray. What a funny name. It took Salmon back to his first day at secondary school: at each new class where he had to give his name for the register, he hoped that the teacher would never reach 'S'. There were always stifled laughs and comments such as 'That's fishy.'

'*T. Pratt!*' Salmon could keep his lips clenched no longer and a broad smile followed the name. 'R. Smith.' Now he could not remove the smile from his face. Smith. What was so funny about Smith? 'Ha ha.' Cough. He paused. 'L. A. Smithson.' He erupted again and tears sprang to his eyes. He coughed, cleared his throat and tried again. He found himself quite unable to read the next name because his mouth was already full. Loud ringing notes and small, choking cries pummelled the insides until his lips felt sore. He was uncontrollably in the grip of the most wonderful laughter. He allowed it to release itself until his whole head relaxed in a paroxysm of total joy. 'I'm sorry . . .

131

I'm sorry . . .' he tried to say in the brief silences when the hysteria paused for breath. But words made it worse. They sounded so funny, so out of place.

There was no expression on any pupil's face during the display. They watched as dispassionately as they might a fairground laughing clown who, owing to their age, they had outgrown and no longer found entertaining. Staff at the end of rows looked carefully along them in the hope of finding something to castigate to divert their attention. Others looked for help towards the stage, where the senior staff appeared to be imprisoned behind bars.

Graystone felt totally helpless. The System laid down no guidelines as to a suitable course of action in such circumstances. Each time he put out his hand, he felt unable to touch the other man, as if afraid that he might receive a severe shock from a highly charged body.

'All right, stop talking,' he said to the school.

The order brought a grateful end to the stillness. As if awakened from a mid-frame stoppage, the pupils began to fidget and whisper amongst themselves. The Head's laughter was reduced to a quiet, slow panting. As it slowed, only the occasional choking noise escaped from the back of his throat, like something clawing for air; but now, it was unaccompanied by a smile. He resumed his seat, folded his hands on his lap and stared at them. The choking began again: at first, only hiccups; but then, like a stone pushed from the top of a hill, it began to roll. As it picked up momentum, each individual sound rolled into one long rhythm of sobbing. Tears ran down his face, each one pulling a little more flesh with it on its journey. His expression melted like wax, and underneath his costume he felt as if he were being withdrawn; his body shrinking to a clenched ball of jelly. Like a dead tortoise whose flesh shrivels, dehydrates and finally disappears, he laid his shell, his graduation gown, over the back of his chair and walked, invisible, away.

Graystone had been waiting twenty years for this moment:

' "They shall grow not old, as we that are left grow old:
Age shall not weary them, nor the years condemn.
At the going down of the sun and in the morning
We will remember them." '

Why did headmasters have all the best lines? Why was it that he, the understudy, had had to wait in the wings, hoping for a broken leg, a heart seizure? But even now, on stage, he knew what they were thinking: he's not as good as the lead; oh, you should have seen it last year.

'I want to talk to you this morning about leaders and heroes,' said Major Barton, beginning his talk. 'I am certain that each of you has someone whom you admire, someone with whom you identify; be it a footballer, a pop star, maybe even one of your own friends . . .'

'I really did object to yew yewsing that pawin,' said Gareth Watts, emphasizing his Welsh accent.

'Which one?' Jonathan Hayward smirked. Every year it was the same.

'Yew do knaw vairy well which one I do mean. That Brooke one: "A body of England's, breathing English air", "the thoughts by England given", "under an English heaven". We was in the war too, yew knaw.'

'I'm sorry, I didn't.'

'Yew . . .'

'Look, Gareth. I'm sorry you don't like the poem, but it happens to be a personal favourite of mine. I'm head of English; I choose the poems. You stick to your metal and guns. Now if you'll excuse me, I'm very busy.'

Watts stormed away. 'Fascist!' he called, followed by what was presumably a tirade of Welsh abuse.

Hayward resumed his marking:

Yesterday was our school memry servise for d Day. The majer said that we must not do any work ourselfs only with others. He said we'd be shot if we mitched off because it was dessersson. And when we go on leave over the summer we should still be good for the school because people will look at us and think thats what the school is like. He said that real hero's don't like themselfs because they want thier freinds to get the glory and real leeders like thier people but some leeders he knows are off thier heads and they should be shot too.

Andrew Kingston 2E

133

It was thought by staff that Grace Calne, being the school's Union representative for ASTHMA (the Area School Teachers and Head Masters' Association), would possess qualities of leadership and organization skills. She had the added advantages of being fifty-five (and therefore responsible), unmarried (and therefore unoccupied), and was therefore elected as official negotiator of the plans for Graystone's retirement dinner. There were invitations, tickets and various contractual agreements to be organized. Food, speeches, wine. Guests, times, seating arrangements. So many considerations underlay the potential success of group dynamics on such evenings, and Grace decided to form a splinter group of the Staff Social Committee to help this along. The news was not well received by the committee's chairman, Alan Richards. He approached the senior mistress when she was pinning up the morning supervision list.

'Uh, Grace, I wonder, could I have a word, please.'

She kept her back to him and busied herself with some minor alterations on the sheet. 'Yes?'

'It's about this . . . uh . . . committee you've formed . . .' Silence. 'I mean, we've already got a social committee. I don't see why you can't deal with us about the dinner. It seems a little ludicrous to form a splinter group when we have a fully elected committee.'

Grace turned to face Richards as if he were a schoolboy who had just uttered an obscenity. 'Does it?' she said, and walked away.

During break, Richards was supervising in the main corridor of the 'old' school. He saw the senior mistress stalking towards him. Boyish fear returned momentarily.

'Mr Richards,' she said, in her normal tone of speech, 'I would be grateful if you did not tell me what I ought and ought not to do in future.'

Richards twitched uneasily. He plucked nervously at his beard with one hand and stroked his hair with the other. Two girls, standing against a radiator, giggled.

'Now just a minute . . .' he started.

Grace's voice became louder. 'If I am appointed to carry out a task, I do it. And I do it without interference from anyone else. Now is that clear?'

Anger and embarrassment made Richards speechless. He watched the senior mistress trot away, stiffly victorious, from her prey. She stopped off at the girls' toilet. Richards heard her low-pitched, hoarse voice admonish some smokers. At the end of break, he went to her room.

'I'm sorry, she's not here,' said Alex Stuart, with whom she shared the room.

The door opened. Grace ignored Richards and sat at her desk. The space between Richards' eyes and the top of his beard went pink, red and then deepened to purple. His voice was low, almost growling, but calm.

'Don't you dare speak to me like that ever again – especially in front of pupils.' His words simmered on the air.

'Have you seen the new Sixth Form time-table?' said Grace, turning to Stuart.

'Did you hear me?' said Richards, raising his voice.

'It was here before break . . .'

Richards leaned over the desk and came to within three inches of the senior mistress's face. 'You'd better hear what I say, because I'm not going to stand for your grossly un-professional conduct.'

'We are exceptionally busy, Mr Richards. Please excuse us.'

'*You!*' shouted Richards, froth lining his lips, 'are everything the kids say you are.' He turned. Grace whitened. 'But you won't get away with it,' he said, turning again at the door and shaking a forefinger at her. 'I'll see that you don't. By God, I will.'

When he had gone, two pink spots appeared beneath Grace's eyes. Alex Stuart continued, in the raw silence, filing record cards.

A material through which electricity flows easily is called a conductor and is said to have a low resistance. Copper is such a material, and for the electrodes Salmon had therefore prepared pieces of copper strip. The wires and cables, through which the current is led, must have an inside core of copper and an outer sheath of rubber or plastic to prevent leakage. There must be a complete conductive path for the current to flow; this is called a circuit and must begin and end at the battery or dynamo. The battery has two poles, the dynamo two terminals. The relay device may be activated by a spring connection, which will briefly delay the current when the push-button is pressed. The current will then travel anti-clockwise, through the coil and back to neutral. This will complete the circuit.

Following his meeting with Grace, Alan Richards went straight to the secretary's office. 'Ken in?' he asked.

Mrs Crashaw rose quickly from her seat and stood sentry at the Head's door. 'He's not seeing anyone.'

'What do you mean, not seeing anyone?'

'Exactly that.' Mrs Crashaw pressed her palms against the length of the door frame.

Zzzzz! A sound similar to that of a dentist's drill came from the other room. Mrs Crashaw bit her lip.

'Look, this is really important,' said Richards. 'I know he's not been well, but . . .'

The secretary stiffened. An expression of 'Don't move, or I'll shoot' entered her eyes.

Richard paused. 'Is he all right?'

'I believe the headmaster is in excellent health and spirits.'

Zzzzz! followed by tap tap tap tap sssss. Silence.

'Trying to make contact with the Russians, is he?' laughed Richards, uneasily.

The secretary did not smile. 'I have not spoken to the Headmaster of late, so I remain totally ignorant of his pursuits.'

'What the hell is going on here? This is supposed to be a school, not the headquarters of the KGB. Now look, I want to see the Head and I want to see him now. And I won't move until I do just that.'

'You'll have a long wait.'

This was worse than trying to get an appointment at the doctor's, thought Richards. Receptionists and secretaries, they ought to be shot.

Zzzzz, mmmmm . . . Silence. Richards waited. Mrs Crashaw knocked on the Head's door.

'I'm busy.'

'I realize that, Mr Salmon. But it's Mr Richards. He's most anxious to see you.'

'I'm busy.'

'I've told him that.'

'Well tell him again.'

'He's here now.'

'I'm busy.'

Richards made a sudden move forward. For several seconds, he and the secretary performed mirror images of each other's movements. Short of using brute physical force, Richards could foresee no method of passing the barrier. He surrendered.

'You're mad!' he called. 'Mad! Every damn one of you. Round the bloody twist! Mad! Mad! Mad!' On his way out, he upset a box of chalk onto the floor. 'Mad!' he said again, and left, slamming the door behind him.

Silence.

'Psst . . . psst!' called the Head. Mrs Crashaw placed her ear against the keyhole of his room. 'Has he gone?'

'Yes, Headmaster, he's gone,' she sighed.

'Good. Good work.' The sound of a heavy object like a piece of furniture made a scraping noise across the floor. 'If anyone else comes, tell them . . . send them to Harold. Harold likes people.'

'Very well, Headmaster. Is there anything else?'

'No, no. That'll be all, thank you.'

Zzzzz. Mmmmm. Silence.

The minutes of Grace's meeting with her sub-committee were posted into pigeon-holes in the SCR. At the top of the sheet was a request to current members of staff to disclose the where-abouts of Riverside's 'deserters'. The minutes contained the information that tickets would be £10 a head for a hot, sit-down meal, prepared by Matron and her cooks, with sherry to start and one bottle of wine between three; extra wine would be available from £4.50 a bottle. The event was to take place between 8.00 p.m. and 12 midnight on July 13, subject to the caretaker's agreement.

Richards was first to his pigeon-hole. 'Ten quid! For the school hall! We could have gone out for less than that. I thought the idea of having it in school was to bring down the cost.'

'Hmph! I suppose we're paying for the governors.'

'One bottle of wine between three!' continued Richards, anxious to find as much wrong with Grace's arrangements as possible. He looked further down the list at the cost of extra wine. Gareth Watts, chairman of the Staff Wine Club, had obviously seen this as an opportunity for a sales increase. '£4.50! We all know who'll be making a profit on that little lot.'

'Oh no, a hot meal,' said Liz Caversham, recently converted to vegetarianism. 'That means it'll be meat and there'll be some ghastly eggy substitute. At least if we'd had a buffet, we could have chosen our own.'

'School bloody hall.'

'Ten quid. Well, my wife won't be coming at that price.'

'I won't be coming at that price!'

'I'll take my own wine.'

'You'll be charged corkage,' said Watts.

Grace entered, only to be serenaded with complaints from all sides.

'Well, you should have put forward proposals if you wanted something different. It's too late now.' More groans. A passer-by might have mistaken their noise for that of an unruly class. 'Gareth has agreed to collect money for the present . . .'

'But he's doing the wine.'

'I can do both.'

'Hey, Gareth – you could give him a crate of wine and keep the 50% discount!'

'Very funny.'

'How much are we supposed to give?'

'Up to you. I'm going to record your names and the amount you give in a book.'

'What!'

'Only so that if you want to, you can pay in instalments.'

'Instalments!'

'Well, Reverend Rock put in £5. Don't tell him I told you, though.'

'I vote we put in a pound for every year we've been here.'

'Then Reverend Rock should have put in £12.'

'All right. A pound for every Scale point.'

'That would put Rocky back down to one. He's never moved.'

138

'Well, I'm not putting in £3,' said John Deignton.

'Three! You didn't tell me you were on Scale 3,' said Nigel Wilton.

'Only kidding,' said Deignton.

Invitations and replies were returned. The final number was to be ninety-one. Now came the most difficult operation – the seating plan.

'Oh, Harold,' said Grace. 'I wonder could you draw up one of your wonderful diagrams. You do them *so* well and I can't really rely on anyone else to get the boxes the right size.'

Graystone consented and Grace sent out another letter to all staff:-

Please list below, in the left-hand column, the names of those with whom you would prefer to be seated upon the occasion of the retirement dinner of Harold G. Graystone, B. A. (Hons.), on July 13. Please state whether you wish them to be on your left or your right side . . .

She had remembered Reverend Rock's partial deafness in his right ear and wanted to make sure he had his first choice seated on his left . . .

. . . or opposite. Please give a second and third choice, also. If your party is larger than ten, please attach a second pro-forma. In the right-hand column, write the names of those with whom you wish especially *not* to be seated (you may include your spouse in this section). Confidences will, of course, be kept. Alternative arrangements can be made for misanthropes.

'I want to sit as far away from her as possible, for a start,' said Alan Richards.

'Just keep Symms away from me,' said Richard Smith.

'I'll sit with you, Dick,' said Katy Ekkart.

For three days, both staff rooms were full of cheer as individuals campaigned for more votes. The JCR opened bets on who was likely to receive the highest number of nominations. Forms were filled in and returned to Grace. She felt a curious sense of power as she went up and down each list. She drew up one of her own and placed ticks alongside names to see who had been given the most votes. Hilary Williams appeared at the top of eight sheets. Grace was sure that some people had been nominating their choices without asking the candidate's permission. Jennifer Sykes, a mere supply, had conveniently been forgotten. There were some highly suspect couplings too - Helen Campbell, the lab. technician, had asked for James McGill on her left and Alan Richards on her right. But James McGill had asked not to be near Liz Caversham who had asked to be opposite Patricia White whom Alan Richards had asked for on his left. Patricia was happy to be near McGill – at least they would be able to talk about Gaelic traditions in the mediaeval lyric, should the evening become boring – but she did not wish to be anywhere near Richards who would, in all likelihood, exploit her position in order to make disparaging remarks about the Arts.

Grace sighed. Here was a form without a name: On my left, I would like Robert Redford; on my right, Donald Duck. Unsigned, of course. And another – opposite the Director of Education. Grace put these aside. This was a far more complex operation than she had originally conceived. A week later, she was still poised tearfully over the plan: fifteen reserved places on the top table and three spines leading from it, two with twenty-five places, one with twenty-six. Tentatively, she began to mark the white spaces with names. Then the moment arrived. Other sheets of paper – notices, brochures and supervision lists (on which Richards' name had been a regular occurrence since his scene with Grace) – were removed from the main notice-board in the SCR in order to give pride of place to what was, in all probability, Graystone's last artistic contribution to Riverside.

The plan was mounted, together with instructions to draw arrows, should anyone wish to change their seat.

'I knew I'd be on a table of duds,' said Deirdre Fraser. 'Just because I'm pregnant.'

'Why didn't you put me on your list?' said Helen Campbell to James McGill. She had been placed with the group that included secretaries, dogsbodies and Miss Beak.

'I did,' he lied.

'I'm not going, now.'

140

'I'm not with one person I asked for,' said Richards.

Five people dropped out completely. Others rockcted arrows in, round and through boxes and names. Graystone stood by, watching the destruction of his work, now smeared with blotches of smudged pencil. As staff manoeuvred themselves away from, or towards the top table – his top table – he shivered. It was as if they were scribbling on his tombstone. When Grace took down the sheet to begin reconstruction work, he felt like a ghost watching his coffin being carried away.

The Hunt

In addition to the excitement of the world of racing, the importance of team spirit can be seen on the day of a big hunt, when riders, horses and hounds come together to participate in one of the most invigorating of activities. All over the county, men and women wake with the smell of blood in their nostrils, anticipating victory. In their dreams, they have galloped through fields, jumped fences and leapt rivers, to the thud of hooves and the yap of hungry hounds. Watching the sun force its way through the gap in the curtains, they listen to the neigh of a horse calling them to rise.

Uniforms have been starched and pressed; buttons polished; hats brushed. Horses have been combed and saddled. Along the route to the meeting-place in the town square, 'Ban Blood-sports' demonstrators and placards are ignored. An impatient motorist beeps his horn; two children wave from the back seat of a bus. A bell rings; they're under starter's orders; and they're off.

Two miles away, a fox slips out from behind a tree from where he has been watching a field of sheep grazing. He runs and runs and runs, sensing the smell of his own blood hot on his heels.

Today, Kenneth Salmon wakes with his head in a press. Feeling nothing but his hands clutching his head, his skull is a globe whose continents he must prevent from spreading into the sea. When he breathes in, his skin rises into his grip; when the breath is released, the muscles in his head contract at the tips of his fingers. He withdraws like a frightened animal hiding in a field. No one can catch him now. Here, it is quiet, rising and falling through breath, hiding in air.

*

'Hey! I just saw Fish Features – in his pyjamas!'

'Get lost.'

'I did. Honest. Top and bottom.'

'Don't believe you . . . what are they like?'

'Blue and White. Stripes. *Honest.*'

'Where's he gone, then?'

'Round by the Sixth Form block. C'mon, I'll show you.'

Rodney Pugh, 3L, led his class-mate, Graham Hart, around the back of the school. It was not yet quarter past eight and the area in question was unpopulated.

'Where? See, I knew you was lyin'.'

'Ssh. Wait.' Rodney held the other boy back and peered around a wall. Suddenly they hit the line, and a bob-tailed figure dressed in blue and white broke covert. Rodney allowed Graham to look. 'See, told you,' he whispered.

Graham watched nervously. His hackles rose. He felt like a character in a horror-movie. 'Is . . . is he real?' He was uncertain as to why he had asked that.

The figure moved forward slowly, the strange clothes seeming to take away his solidity.

'C'mon, let's go,' said Graham, turning to run the heel way.

'Don't be daft.'

'Look, he's coming closer.'

'Don't be stupid, he can't hurt you.'

The two boys came out into the clear ground and showed themselves. Rodney's laughter had given way to a sort of fear, though he dared not admit to it. The figure came to within a few feet of them but seemed to be unaware of their presence.

'He's coming for us . . . let's run,' said Graham, though he found himself unable to move.

It was clear that the Head had no intention of stopping and the boys were forced to jump out of the way. They watched the somnambulant figure enter the back yard, where other pupils coupled together, panting and laughing. Rodney hated their stares. This event had been his challenge and he had wanted to spread the story like the Messenger in the play they were doing in English. His Scoop was not meant for this mocking laughter. Whatever response he had hoped for he was uncertain; but he knew that this was not it. They had missed some essential element in the story itself; misinterpreted the spectacle they

142

saw before them. Rodney fought back anger and frustration towards them. What he wanted was some kind of understanding – of what, exactly, he didn't know; the opportunity to share his fear of this thing for which he couldn't find a word.

At the bicycle sheds, Salmon stopped and registered for the first time several pairs of curious eyes. He waited a few seconds, matching their stares with his own frightened eyes. They had trapped him. Driven him to this spot while others advanced upon him from behind. Soon he would be surrounded. There was only one thing to do. And he ran.

The pupils, carrying a good head, instinctively followed and started to run. They must not lose sight of their prey. They would course him and bring him, exhausted, back to their own territory. There they would break-up and share him out among their hungry mouths.

'There he goes!' shouted a girl, glimpsing a sudden cloud of blue and white. 'Run! Run! Faster! Faster!'

Several other pupils tagged on to the group when it passed. Coursing their victim, the scent of a kill spurred them on.

Salmon paused and leaned against a wall, listening for the music of his pursuers. They were gaining on him. He had to find his way back to earth. There they would not be able to cast him. He padded quietly towards the main building. He had lost a slipper in the chase, and with every step small stones buried themselves in his right sole. He stopped to pick them out.

'Holloa!' came a shout, followed again by the thunder of footsteps and the cry of hunger.

The pupils, inspired by the sight of their fox, picked up speed and ran mute. Ties and blazers were discarded as sweat broke out, making shirts cling to bodies, hackles stand on end. Now they had really caught the scent and would not lose it again. On and on they ran, through bottoms and coverts, and on and on went Salmon, never daring to glance behind. Suddenly the playing fields came to an end and Salmon found himself trapped. Several yards the other side was the river – but how to reach it? Gathering up the last of his strength, he broke covert, tearing his pyjamas and his skin as he did so. There was no time for pain and he stumbled towards the water. Rolling down the bank, stiff and exhausted, he finally submerged his heat in the

143

cool river. Along the bank, the hounds marked the ground, casting the lost scent.

When he was sure they had given up and returned to school, Salmon hauled himself out of the water and crawled up the bank. The river being shallow at this point, he was wet only to his knees, though he felt the chill right through his body. In the distance, he heard the first bell of the morning and the movement of voices as pupils made their way inside.

He had a straight run to his room. If he hurried, he could reach it while the rest of the school was in registration; climb in through the window he had left unlocked in the stock-room. He reached it and clambered through, as the buzzer for morning assembly sounded in his office. He tried to calm his breathing, patted his chest as if soothing it to sleep; slowly, he felt warmth and stillness retuning to his cold, wet body. Recognising his state of dress for the first time, it struck him not with strangeness or fear, but as a simple reminder of something he had forgotten to do. He sat at his desk, laid his wet hands, palms facing upwards, in front of him, and waited.

CHAPTER EIGHT

OUT OF THE RACE

The competitive sport of racing is a particularly demanding one, in which success is dependent upon many factors. Among the most common causes of the failure of a horse to complete a course are sudden injury (e.g. falling at a fence) and general fatigue. If, however, a jockey is thrown from his/her horse, the animal is allowed to finished the race itself, though cannot be awarded a prize. External factors – weather, track conditions etc. – can also affect the performance of any individual on the big day.

Breaking the Circuit

It needed no electrical genius to decipher the code that operated the school bell and buzzer system. Set in a small black box in the Head's study and run from the mains electricity supply, Kenneth Salmon was struck by the simplicity of the device. What surprised him was the fact that no one had before carried out this act of sabotage he was about to commit. He rolled up his pyjama sleeves and examined the contents of the box more closely. Essential to the smooth running of the establishment's organization and routine, surely it was obvious that by disconnecting the coloured wires, each attached to a number or label, the establishment would no longer be able to function as normal. With no signal, there could be no orders from staff telling their pupils to stand, sit, walk or shut up. No more demands of a clock face; no more sun crossing his window at the time when the bell normally went for lunch: the visual and verbal reminders of the fact that he still had half a day to go. It would mean the end of timetables. Routines. Races. The end of school time. All he had to do was break the circuit. He had completed the course, and won. At last he would be free.

Jonathan Hayward stood in the men's toilet in the SCR, his left hand resting against the white tiles on the wall above the urinal, his right holding his inert, dry penis. Was it God's punishment for his having avoided assembly for the third time that week? If only the bell would ring for first lesson. His bladder was fuller than it had ever been, he was certain. Half a jug of milk on his corn flakes, two mugs of tea *and* a glass of water before he left home this morning; it had to be full. Besides, he could feel it, and he always disposed of a lot between assembly and first lesson. It was an established routine that he, his bladder and the bell had grown well accustomed to over the years.

'Trrring! Trrring! . . . *Trrrrring!*' Hayward attempted an imitation of the bell in the hope that his bladder would be unable to distinguish the difference in tone. It could. '*Brrr* . . . *Brrr* . . .' he tried, a little lower. But not a drop.

Theme for Morning Assembly: What is an Angel?

Alison Hayman (4A) has been gorging herself. Please would all staff who teach her keep a careful watch. Gorging could be a sign of anorexia.

With reference to the obscene phone-calls made earlier this term to girls in Form Five. The police have traced the culprit but he is, thankfully, not a member of this school.

Mr and Mrs Gray (parents of Ian, Upper Sixth) have donated £50 to the school as a token of appreciation for their son's education. Staff are requested to emphasise to pupils our appreciation of such gestures.

Regarding house points. It has been reported by pupils in Form Three that some teachers awarded 10 points to pupils who agreed to participate in a house assembly. Staff are reminded that three is the maximum number of points to be given at any one time.

Staff are asked to pay for *all* telephone calls.

Sandwiches must *not* be eaten at the front of the school. Litter is again becoming a problem.

David Howells (3L), who was rushed into hospital last night, is reported to be suffering from a brain tumour. Staff are requested to be patient with Ann (1S), his sister, who is under considerable strain.

I hereby submit my notice of the post Photocopier Attendant, following more complaints regarding problems with the machine. As I myself never have any trouble using it, I feel I can no longer be sympathetic to the increasing demands being made upon my services. It is with great regret that I have reached this decision.

Harold G. Graystone

No more bets can be taken on the outcome of the final interviews for the post of Deputy-Head. The odds stand as follows:-

Alex Stuart 6–4 FAV
Grace Calne 100–1 against

Grace Calne ripped the last notice from the board, added the morning's supervision list and posted a few letters into pigeon-holes while she waited for the bell to ring for first lesson. Assembly had been a great success and although the pupils were ten times more confused about angels than they had been before, she certainly was not. Suddenly, with Damascus-like clarity, she saw that every living being possessed his/her own angel. So powerful was this new sense of goodness within her at that moment, she could almost feel two wings sprouting in her shoulder blades, a golden light starting to form about her head. What is an Angel? 'Speak, Lord, thy servant heareth,' she answered.

But the bell did not ring. Grace looked at her watch. It was 9.35. Lessons should have started five minutes ago. She sat down.

'Shouldn't you all be in lessons?' she asked nobody in particular. 'The bell went five minutes ago,' she lied, in the hope that this would stir at least a few.

Nobody moved.

'Maybe we should go anyway,' said Andrew Young, though he found himself unable to move.

'It was working for registration and assembly,' said Grace. She was thinking of all the blazer-less pupils she was missing.

'What will we do if it doesn't go?'

Some looked around in horror. Others looked pleased that they would miss lessons.

In the JCR, Geoff Symms clung to the *Telegraph*. 'Suits me,' he said. 'I hate 3E anyway.'

Graystone, who had popped in only to deliver a message, was angry at finding himself trapped in the less desirable staff room.

'Well, you know what Samuel Butler says,' he announced, ' "Time is the only purgatory." '

Appropriate though the sentiment was, staff ignored it. If purgatory was anything, it was being confined to the same room as Graystone, thought Malcolm Hewitt.

Half an hour passed and at 10.05, the atmosphere in both staff rooms became tense as they waited for a signal calling them to second lesson.

Jonathan Hayward changed hands and tried to shake his penis into urination, as if he were operating a stirrup-pump. His eyes were screwed tightly shut and his lower lip bled where he had bitten into it in his agony. His pumping was useless and he tried again to sing the note of the bell. Now, he could utter nothing but a high-pitched squeak. All the rivers, swimming-pools and running taps he brought to mind could offer no relief. Surely, this was hell.

Esther Lamb, taking her regular morning jog around the school running track, had now been going for an hour. Normally, in the time between assembly and first lesson, she passed the trees by the river only twice; today, she had already counted six times and still the school bell had not beckoned her to work. Soaked in sweat and with aching legs, she again tried to stop, but her legs ignored her mind's request. Tick tock tick tock tick tock – her feet hit the ground with monotonous regularity and here again were the trees by the river.

'Ladies and gentlemen,' said Graystone, 'there is nothing to stop us all just standing up, walking to the door and going to our classrooms. Our pupils are, after all, expecting us.'

'Go on, then,' said Geoff Symms.

'Very well.'

Graystone made a few tentative steps towards the door and stopped.

'Not as easy as you thought, is it?' said Symms.

'The handbell!' said Graystone, struck with an idea. 'Where is it?'

'The office.'

'Then all we have to do is contact the secretary by telephone, ask her to ring the bell and then we can all get back to work.'

Graystone suddenly felt in control, the James Bond of the situation. He picked up the telephone and rang through to the office.

'Ah, Dorothy, Harold here. We have a small problem and were wondering if you could do us a favour. You see, we need you to ring the handbell . . . that's right . . . What's that? . . . But all you have to do is pick it up . . . but it's *gone* 9.30 . . . but that's not our fault . . . I see . . . Very well.' He hung up.

'I'm afraid the secretary . . . uh . . . as you know . . . does not start answering requests until 9.30 and . . . uh . . . as the bell did not go at 9.30, she has no way of knowing when she should start.'

'Can't she look at her bloody watch?' said Hewitt.

'You know as well as I do, Mr Hewitt, that once in school, we operate by the bell,' said Graystone. 'Watches cannot be trusted.'

Reverend Rock liked to thank God for the inspirational talks he gave at assembly. For ten minutes each day, he went down on

149

bended knees to talk with his Maker, before tackling once again the sheep and goats. This morning his back had started to ache and his knees were sore. When he tried to raise himself, he was unable to move. Maybe God disagreed with his Angel theory. It was only a *theory* though, he reassured. Not to be taken *too* seriously. Next time, he would stick more literally to the text, he promised. But trapped as he now was, like so many God-fearing men before him – Samson in the temple, Paul in prison, Jonah in the whale – Reverend Rock could only wait for a sign.

Completing the Circuit

Kenneth Salmon tested the relay switch once more and noted with satisfaction the delayed response of the main circuit. He was proud of the chair he had constructed. At last, all the wires in place, the additional pieces of wood set firm, he tested it and sat, king of his castle, listening to the silence all around. Now he could go away in peace. He strapped in his feet, his chest and his head so that they touched their corresponding electrodes. His hands he slid under the wrist straps, as far as they would go until he felt his arms lock into place; his fingers lock against another set of copper electrodes. Each of the terminals, four live and four neutral on opposite sides of his body, were linked by single core, bare copper solder wires; their positive and negative forces joined at the secondary winding, wound two thousand times. The current would arrive at this point, via the primary winding and the contactor, which would operate from the main circuit.

And with my hand over the switch I am taking possession. With my hand on the switch I am taking total control. Press the switch – and the fingers of that hand tremble in air – no clawing muscle now – and numb – Frantic pulsing in every limb – this thing feeding every cell of my blood – blood rocking so fast I feel it break – Pinball body – balls of blood shooting round – Ends of my veins – balls of blood fighting to go first – everything fighting for the ends of my veins – and finding more – so many ends – Whole body an exit – and this thing sawing to get out –

150

Back arched – breaking – wrists burning – feet stiff – head swollen – cheeks balloons – eyeballs travelling my face – mouth forced open – Body open – Exits all opened – Crowds rushing through – Too many clamouring for the exit – Keep calm – Don't panic – But the crowds – trampling – Being crushed to death inside – Trampled underfoot – A second's silence – And doors close.

When Graystone looked at his watch, it was mid-day. The lights in the JCR flickered on and off for several seconds, before going out completely. Suddenly, the staff room was in darkness.

'Ah, the lights are going out all over Europe,' said Graystone, a little shaky on Light and Shade quotations.

'How much longer are we going to have to sit here?' asked Hewitt, as if suspecting Graystone of having engineered the whole operation.

'Patience, Mr Hewitt. Patience.'

There was silence again, as if in the darkness they expected something significant to occur at last. Jonathan Hayward remained in the toilet of the SCR in a state of penial rupture; Esther Lamb, with severe cramp, kept on running; while Reverend Rock recited the Act of Contrition. Kenneth Salmon sat in his electric chair, no longer conscious of the power which governed his body.

'Headmaster! Headmaster!' called Dorothy Crashaw, knocking at the door. She tried the handle but it was, as usual, locked.

And as suddenly as darkness had fallen, then there was light. And with that light, the loud, joyful ringing of a bell. Reverend Rock praised God, and Esther Lamb collapsed. The heavenly sound flowed through Jonathan Hayward like water over an arid plain, and in the SCR toilet, water began to flow into the arid urinal as his bladder gave way.

'To lessons! To lessons!' shouted Grace Calne, rushing into the corridor. 'You, girl! Where's your blazer!'

'The Headmaster . . .' panted Mrs Crashaw, finding Graystone in the JCR. '. . . I think there's something most dreadfully wrong.'

Graystone, Hewitt and Symms followed her back to the office.

151

'. . . Awful . . . Noises . . .' she tried again, but finding that the words would not come, just pointed to Salmon's door.

'It's locked,' said Graystone, trying the handle.

'I'll go round,' said Hewitt.

Finding the open window through which Salmon had climbed to escape his pursuers, Hewitt entered the study. Salmon's pale face, tinged only by the blue in his swollen lips, took him by surprise. Several burnt wires hung from a home-made transformer beside the chair on the floor. Hewitt walked as far as possible around the body and unlocked the door.

'You'd better call an ambulance,' he instructed Mrs Crashaw.

'My God,' said Symms.

'Coats,' said Graystone. 'As many as possible. To keep him warm.' He felt Salmon's quick and feeble pulse, his cold clammy skin. 'And tea – lots of it, with plenty of sugar.'

Graystone and Symms laid Salmon out on the floor and raised his legs onto a small stool. When the ambulance arrived, he was lifted onto a stretcher. He opened his eyes, just long enough to take in the blurred figure of Graystone, and closed them again.

So, then, he had not won. The school bell continued to ring in every room and the race went on. He was the injured, having to be carried from the track. He clung tightly to a hand – maybe it was his own. Would they now have to shoot him, after all? He squeezed his eyes more tightly shut and waited for the press of cold metal against his head.

The Last Lap

'. . . And some of you will go on to be doctors and lawyers. Others will become brain surgeons, vets, politicians . . . and there's a place in the world for the rest of you, too,' said Gerald Leigh, Director of Education.

The school had gathered in the Sports hall for final assembly. Leigh had been called in as guest speaker to say farewell to Graystone.

'Now your deputy-head, I don't mind telling you, is a bit of an academic,' he went on. 'I was talking to an ex-tutor of his the

152

other day who told me that he *should* have got a First Class degree at university.' He paused for the strength of this claim to sink in. 'And he's a man who has used that intelligence in your service.

'You see, children . . . I think I can say that I know a bit about education by now . . . and I'm reminded today of the very first Headmaster of this school, Dr Edwards. None of you will remember him, of course, but he was a man who fulfilled his great ambition and died very suddenly. He always said that a good school was like a well-run ship, and to run that ship, it was important to have an Alpha man.

'Well . . . uh . . . Mr Salmon is, of course, the captain, but we must always be grateful to Mr Graystone for being such a good mate. He's been a faithful servant of the school, both in the grammar school days and then in this bisexual school.

'But "last" is a terrible word. I can hardly bear to utter that final combustible consonant, bespeaking in itself a staccato shekinah of finality. But I must. When the winds blow to hurricane intensity, their dying down is inevitable. Yet the wind of Harold Graystone is something we will never forget. We wish him well for his retirement, and as our ship moves on, we wave from the deck, saying not goodbye, but *au revoir.*'

Leigh, waving from the deck, lowered his arm and feeling pleased with his performance, looked around the hall. There wasn't a dry seat in the house, he told his wife.

The school hall had been decorated with red, white and blue (Graystone had always been a great patriot), and from the stage, the voices of the James Last Singers floated softly thought two black speakers that had been borrowed (at a small fee) from the Music department. Roses and fern made up each of the flower arrangements on the tables and were laid alternately between candles in silver sticks. Matron had insisted that her cooks have their uniforms freshly laundered and starched for the occasion, and at 5.30 an after-school lingerer or reconnoitring spy would have observed a snow-white row of ghosts lining up in the hall for inspection.

Matron had taken several weeks to choose her menu. Alex Stuart was allergic to cheese, Julia Soames could not eat white

153

meat, and there were three staff and two guests who were vegetarians. Well, they would just have to be content with an inferior meal. If they were going to be awkward, that was their look-out. Vegetarianism. A lot of stuff and nonsense. There'd been no such thing years ago. No herbivores then! No homosexuals either. There must be a connection, she thought.

The carnivores would undoubtedly be getting better value for their money, and to add that little bit of extra excitement to the evening, Matron offered a prize (a copy of her unpublished manuscript, *Gastric Intercourse*) for the person who came the closest to guessing the symbolic relevance of the menu to Graystone's own life. She had remembered snippets of gossip from over the years; for more private information, she consulted other sources – Graystone's friends, ex-colleagues; even his wife, Barbara, on one small matter. She knew that most people would immediately recognise something French about the food, though the fish pâté was only red herring. The exotic French tart with black cherries was the real clue – but whose memory would travel as far back as The Incident itself? The secretary, who took all those phone calls from Paris? The main course, stuffed breast of lamb, could be interpreted in several ways: Graystone's enemies might say it symbolised his lack of a real heart; the literal-minded would say it was a mere representation of his weakness in that area; but only She – She who had travelled three miles to the Infirmary to check upon the reasons for Graystone's recent visits, She who had bribed the Sister into disclosing confidential information – only She would know that the stuffed breast was a symbol of Graystone's pacemaker, the subject of which he had never discussed. The petits pois could only be guessed if the first part of the French theme were fully discovered – *all those tiny seeds ripped from their pods before they were fully grown.* The final touch was a potato in its jacket – the skin decorated with a checked pattern, the design of which had been copied from the jacket Graystone had worn for the greater part of his teaching career.

Graystone stood in front of the dressing-table mirror, hoisted up his trousers and gathered the superfluous material under his belt. It was two years since he had worn his evening suit and he

154

felt a little sad at the amount of solid flesh his low-fat diet had caused him to lose. It had become so much a part of him, both literally and metaphorically, that as each pound slipped away he felt a pang such as the loss of virility brings. He had bought a new dickie bow for this occasion and gave the wings of the fat, black velvet butterfly a final tug, before standing back to admire his appearance as a whole.

'There!' he combed his small moustache and tuft of beard. His remark was intended to indicate the finality of his actions, a signal for him to turn his back and go downstairs. Yet he found himself unable to leave the room. He remained in front of the mirror: the more he stared, the more ridiculous his reflection appeared, the visual equivalent of an everyday word we repeat over and over until it loses its meaning. He sat on the stool and fingered his wife's small pots and jars of various creams littering the top; he made a clean finger-trail through a pale brown spillage of face powder, as if to reassure himself of physical reality. When he turned again to the mirror, it occurred to him that he had the kind of face that looked as if it might easily go out.

Barbara, his wife, returned from the bathroom. 'Come on, Harold. It's time to go.' She gave her hair, specially whisked into a bouffant, a vigorous spray. 'You are ready, are you?'

'Of course.' Graystone frowned. He was always ready first, wherever they went, but allowed his wife her little routine. It had been the same for the whole of their married life, yet tonight he was irritated by it. Earlier in the evening, he had stepped out of the bath onto one of her toe-nails – a small half-moon, hard and sharp – and he had hated it. He picked it from his flesh as delicately as he had once removed splinters from his children's skin; he laid it in his palm and hated everything from which that nail had grown. After thirty-five years of marriage, he hated his wife for cutting her toe-nails on the bathroom carpet. And at the same time, he feared the tiny rim. Its sudden incision into his bare foot was a reminder of her; he feared the time he would now be forced to spend with a person who was little more than a stranger: the strangeness that comes with a sense of over-familiarity; knowing someone sufficiently well to the point of forgetting their immediate presence. Ten minutes will now pass, he thought; she will change her ear-rings twice;

155

she will hold several pendants and chains against the front of her dress; she will ask his opinion and finally decide upon the opposite; she will wrap a shawl around her shoulders and say, with a touch of kindly impatience in her voice. 'Come *on*, Harold. Why are you always last?'

He had timed it to perfection, as usual. But still he could not move from the seat.

'You're feeling all right, are you?'

'Mm . . . fine,' he answered. 'I was just thinking . . . you know, I mean . . . all those years . . .' he corrected himself – '. . . terms.' He made a quick calculation of the number of terms he had taught, multiplying the number of years by three, as he might calculate a dog's age with the multiple of seven. There were well over a hundred. When he shuts his eyes, he can open and close the memories like a breath of air. If he holds them a moment too long, they rush from him in a quick exhalation he is unable to stop. So he regulates each thought and draws them in to the count of ten, holds, and releases them to the count of five. He breathes back further than ten to a sense of water running on glass across his past. To bring these distant memories into focus, he fills them with the breath that is full of him; stretches them to the perfect tautness of balloon skin. When they let him out, he breathes them back again. 'It's been a long time.'

'Oh, Harold. Now don't start going all morbid. Be thankful that Ken's going to be all right, at least. This is supposed to be a happy occasion. Goodness only knows, you all need cheering up. You're retiring. Just think – all those things you've always wanted to do; now you'll be free to do them. You'll be able to spend more time in the garden, go fishing, play golf . . .'

Suddenly, the vision of open air and open spaces fills Graystone with a sense of panic: the garden, where he can dig deeper and deeper until he reaches the centre of the earth; the river, beside which he can sit with all the time in the world to catch nothing: watch the water steal his memories, carry them a little further downstream each day and finally hook him, an indifferent fish, from the bank; and the golf course, where he will now have the time to look for that lost ball under dry leaves. At last he had reached the age at which he could be offered the ultimate prize: the dimension and space of childhood, that stretches down to the centre of the earth, is carried away to the sea, and travels way up over the last green. But he felt cheated. Why had he been offered this space now? Was it because they knew he no longer had need of it? Because they knew that once let out, he would crawl into the shade, having been thrust, after too long a period inside, into a new world? The prize, his golden handshake, was nothing more than an illusion. When they finally scoop him out, he will go into the garden, dig a small hole at the foot of a tree and cover himself with leaves. He will nestle up against the hard pillow of a golf-ball lost in the undergrowth.

'Let's have a look at you, then.' Barbara pulled her husband to his feet.

'Do . . . do I look all right?' Graystone stood to face his wife, his eyes beckoning approval like those of a child in his first school uniform.

'You look lovely.' Barbara stood on tip-toe and kissed his cheek. He shrank slightly, by instinct rather than intention, from the touch of her lips, a small boy having reached the age when an adult's kiss is cause for embarrassment. He resented the fact that it had been delivered as a kiss of hope and survival, rather than affection; when what he wanted, more than anything else at that moment, was to crawl into hibernation.

To the Slaughter

'The old grammar schools taught you D & C – Discipline and Courtesy!' said Gerald Leigh. They employed teachers with D & C – Degrees and Common Sense, while the others . . .' (Dregs and Charlatans, he thought) '. . . were employed by the sec mods.'

Jonathan Hayward, sitting next to the Director of Education, had had enough of this If I Ruled the World talk. 'Excuse me,' he interrupted, 'you have some tomato pips on your chin.'

'Oh . . . er . . . thank you,' said Leigh, wiping his face.

'Do go on, Gerald,' said his wife.

'Where was I? . . . Ah, yes. Single sex grammar schools – just the ticket. Brought you up with the right idea that girls were

157

girls and boys were boys. None of this feminist nonsense, boys doing Cookery, girls doing Woodwork.'

'Just because I'm pregnant, there's no need to be sexist,' said Deirdre Fraser.

'Less unemployment then, too,' said Mrs Solomon-Myne, a governor.

'And more God,' said Reverend Rock.

' " There are three wants which can never be satisfied," ' said Graystone to his small audience on the top table. 'Ralph Waldo Emerson. "That of the rich who wants something more; that of the sick who wants something different; and that of the traveller who says, Anywhere but here!" '

'Ho ho ho,' around the table.

'You see,' said Leigh,' the sec. mods with the CSEs didn't get ideas above their station. They took what they were offered, accepted what they were paid for doing it and were grateful for it. Then the better positions were left for those coming out of the grammars, the ones with the brains, those who knew how a country should be run.'

'People such as yourself,' said Hayward.

'Well, yes, I suppose so.'

'You were looked up to if you went to a grammar school,' said Mrs Leigh.

'Quite right,' said her husband, nodding approvingly. 'Prefects meant something then, too. Head boy was Somebody – head girl, even. But then what do they go and do? Mix them all up together. and then what happens? Practically a revolution. All these kids who've never even heard of 'O' Levels now think they're being cheated in some way.'

'They are,' said Hayward.

'Well . . . yes . . . But we don't have to make them aware of it.'

'Too much knowledge is a bad thing,' warned Mrs Leigh.

'And not enough God,' said Reverend Rock.

'Especially if it's placed in the wrong hands,' said Leigh. 'Keep them ignorant, that's what I say. But no. Now they're not happy with their Grade 1 CSE – If it's the same as 'O' Level, why can't I do the 'O' Level? they say. Well, that's what you teachers must expect if you're going to try and pull the wool over their eyes and tell them you're doing it. They've

158

just moved a bit further down the bottle, that's all. You can't be the cream for ever.'

'Lovely pâté,' said Liz Caversham to a cook serving at her table.

'Red herring,' she said.

'Excuse me,' said Hayward, 'I need a piss.'

'Well, really,' whispered Mrs Leigh to her husband.

'D & C, like I said,' he nodded.

Hayward smirked.

'Next course,' announced Matron, standing sentry at the kitchen hatch.

Plates of meat and dishes of vegetables quickly filled up tables.

'It's a shame that Ken couldn't have been here,' said Graystone.

'Mor - bid - Har - old,' said Barbara, through a smile, and kicking her husband under the table.

'I just feel that we could have – *should* have done something sooner. I mean, we knew that something was up. He must have been all right at home or Jo would have . . . *Ow!* . . . *Mmm*, this looks tasty.'

'Bad luck about the job, Grace,' called Alan Richards.

Grace Calne, sitting on the next table, pretended not to hear.

'This Ron Halliday's a good friend of mine,' he went on. 'I think he'll be very good. Knows how to handle people.'

'Senior Mistress carries just as much weight as Deputy Head,' said Grace. 'More than Head of Department, anyway.'

'And that,' smiled Richards, 'is why you'll still be here in twenty years – and I won't.' He turned back to his own table of friends and left Grace, blushing, to her stuffed breast.

'That Mr Young looks drunk already,' said Mrs Leigh. 'And if that's his wife, she looks positively obscene in that dress.'

Gerald Leigh smiled approvingly at his wife's tubular dress, covering her completely from neck to ankle.

'Well, it hurt for a few days,' said Symms, 'but I think, on the whole, the advantages outweigh the disadvantages.'

'Means you can screw around more easily, eh Geoff!' said Andrew Young.

'Less messy, I imagine,' said his wife.

'Oh no,' said Symms, taking large gulps of wine. 'You see, it's only the sperm that gets stopped, not the semen.'

'I see,' said Mrs Young.

'Hundred calories a mouthful,' said her husband.

'I'm sorry?'

'Semen – hundred calories a mouthful. Fact, that.'

'Oh dear,' said Mrs Symms.

Matron walked around each table, supervising her cooks' serving of the main meal.

'You've excelled yourself,' said Graystone, squeezing her arm. 'This meat looks done to perfection.'

'Only the best for you, Mr Graystone. And I've trimmed the fat specially.'

'That's a very nice dress you're wearing,' said Symms to Mrs Young.

'Don't drink too much, Geoff,' warned his wife. 'I'm not going to drive you home in a state.'

'You have *never* had to drive me home in a state. As I recall . . .'

'Not now, Geoff.'

'Threw up all over Jennifer Daley's fur coat, as I remember.'

'I said, *not now*, Geoff.'

'Then they found the other half of it a month later – in a flowerpot! Had to have the greenhouse fumigated.'

'I'm warning you, Geoff . . .'

'No thank you,' said Hayward. 'I'm one of the vegetarians.'

'No meat for me,' said Liz Caversham.

'There's plenty more if anyone wants it,' said Matron.

'It really is quite delicious.'

'The meat's so tender.'

'So juicy too.'

'Done to a treat.'

'I'd love some more.'

'Me too.'

'Yes, please. More for this table as well.'

Matron returned to the kitchen. Seconds later, she came back with one of the larger school canteen double-decker trolleys. On it, amid parsley trims and fresh fruit, lay a half-eaten carcass, still steaming with hot, tender flesh.

'Oh my,' said Mrs Leigh, 'how very beautiful.'

All heads turned. Graystone gave a standing ovation and others followed suit, clapping. Matron blushed.

'Well I'm damned,' said Gerald Leigh. 'You certainly fooled me. Could have sworn it was lamb. More! More!'

Shouts and cheers hailed the decapitated sacrificial animal, which lay on its back on the trolley; its four legs, hoofs well polished and decorated with small chef's hats, stuck straight up. From the bottom half of the trolley, Matron produced a silver salver, covered with a large silver dome. Holding it aloft, she carried it to Graystone on the top table and laid it, ceremoniously, before him. Slowly, he removed the lid. His eyes met a large eye, staring out from a brown, shining head.

'It's real crystal,' said Matron, glowing.

Silence ruled in the hall as staff and guests gathered round to admire the horse's head, complete with real crystal eye.

'It really is quite, quite beautiful,' said Graystone, smoothing the sleek hair.

'Horsemeat. Never have guessed it in a million years,' said Leigh, taking advantage of the distraction to pull a piece of breast from the carcass.

Graystone was deeply moved. Matron, sensitive to the embarrassment of the situation, stirred the silence.

'Come along now, come up with your plates. There's plenty more for everyone.'

A long queue quickly formed and plates were once again piled high with greater helpings of horsemeat. The vegetarians looked on with distaste.

'There'll be none left by the time it gets to us,' moaned Malcolm Hewitt at the back of the queue. 'I vote we just go and grab our own meat.'

'Hear! Hear!'

'Forward!'

Hewitt led the crush to the front of the queue. Reverend Rock, struggling with a leg, was thrust aside. Others who had been usurped fought back, punching and kicking in any direction. Hewitt, losing balance, grabbed a leg. Someone pushed him from behind and he clung on more desperately. He heard the slow creaking of bones coming apart at the joint as the leg fell to his weight.

'Look what I've got!' he shouted, finding his way out of the crush and waving a leg in the air.

'And me!' called Geoff Symms, joining him for a leg and hoof duel.

161

'Stop! Stop!' called Matron. 'One at a time, please.'

But it was too late. Fruit, parsley and bone went flying, as more guests, fearing that they would miss out on seconds, dived for the horse.

' "A horse! A horse! My kingdom for a horse!" ' shouted Graystone, rushing in and spearing a flank with his knife.

Now they were ruthless in their attempts, diving in and tearing at any piece of the animal's flesh which came to hand. It no longer mattered whether it was breast or leg; everything found its way into their greedy mouths as they stuffed their faces with the same relish as Matron had earlier stuffed the horse's head.

'Look what I've found!' shouted Leigh, waving roast testicles in the air.

Reverend Rock, on his feet again, reached for them, but in his haste fell against the trolley. Over it went, sending the few remaining pieces of flesh and bone right across the room.

'I saw them first!'

'No, you didn't,' said Leigh, chewing a ball.

Soon there was no more flesh to be seen. Bones littered the floor, and the satisfied licked their lips and wiped their greasy faces.

'I'm full,' burped Graystone.

'Me, too.'

'An excellent meal, Matron. Most satisfying.'

'Horsemeat. Well I'm damned,' said the Director of Education.

Kenneth Salmon woke again and took in the unfamiliar surroundings. He needed air. Why did they have to lock his windows – and the door? He couldn't breathe properly. He was sweating. It was the same dream which had woken him again. Each time he opened his eyes, he felt both surprise and panic at the fact that he was still alive; surprise that they had let him off, after all; and panic that they would most certainly try to get him again.

In the dream, he is running – not in a field or on a track, nor in a race; just running through an empty space: no people, no buildings, nothing around him. There is no sense of urgency in the dream. He is not frightened, but runs as if there is no other course open to him, as if this is what he has always done and must inevitably go on doing. But something stops him. Suddenly he cannot run and he knows he will fall through the space. He finds himself in a white room. He can hear them moving around but he cannot see them. Who are they? It's the best thing, he hears them say. Quickly. In the head. He feels cold metal pressed against his temple. Now, he hears them say. Now. But the shot never comes.